THE HAUNTING OF HELEN WREN

THE HAUNTING OF HELEN WREN

Jan Alexander

This Large Print book is published by BBC Audiobooks Ltd, Bath, England and by Thorndike Press®, Waterville, Maine, USA.

Published in 2004 in the U.K. by arrangement with the author.

Published in 2004 in the U.S. by arrangement with Wieser & Elwell, Inc.

U.K. Hardcover ISBN 0–7540–9926–1 (Chivers Large Print)
U.S. Softcover ISBN 0–7862–6493–4 (General)

The text of this Large Print edition is unabridged.
Other aspects of the book may vary from the original edition.

Set in 16 pt. New Times Roman.

Printed in Great Britain on acid-free paper.

British Library Cataloguing in Publication Data available

Library of Congress Control Number: 2004101134

PROLOGUE

Doctor, she said, before she said anything else, *I am haunted. By ghosts.*

It was little wonder, too, after what had happened to her.

PART ONE

HELEN

CHAPTER ONE

A man and a woman were playing tennis, energetically but not well. From three separate windows above, three women watched them. The women in the windows were not acquainted, nor connected, except that life had brought them simultaneously to this point. Their three windows were as close as they would ever come to one another, and when they moved away from them, their paths would not cross again.

One of the watchers was thinking of some bad news she had just received. Another was thinking of a man who had made love to her once, and whose hair was the color of the man's on the tennis court. The third was thinking of blood, of the smell of it, and the feel of it, warm and wet and sticky, and the sight of it, crimson, staining clothes and flesh.

'Miss Wren?'

Helen turned from the window. One of the nurses was standing in the open door. She was dressed not in the traditional nurse's white, but in a ghastly pink pants-uniform; the outside of this building was pink, too, and even the walls of the room in which she stood were a paler shade of pink. Helen had sometimes felt as if she were trapped in a web of cotton candy.

'Your sister is waiting,' the nurse said.

Helen made a pretense of a smile and came with the nurse out of the room, along the corridor toward the lobby. She was very nervous, but she had had many years experience of not showing what she felt. She wanted to run, but she kept her pace perfectly matched to the short, quick little steps of the nurse.

'Doctor Ida wants to see you before you go,' the nurse said, slowing the pace as they neared the open door of the doctor's office.

Helen stopped, feeling as if she had been tricked. 'I thought I had been released,' she said accusingly.

'He only wants to tell you goodbye,' the nurse said, indicating the open door. 'He always tells his patients goodbye, and wishes them luck.'

Helen came in, pausing just inside the door. The doctor was seated behind his big desk, facing the door. He did not rise when she came in, but smiled a greeting. She had never liked his smile.

'Helen,' he said, making it a complete sentence. 'So, you're going to leave us.'

She said, very softly, almost prayerfully, 'Yes.'

'We'll miss you, you know.' He paused, but when she made no reply to that, he went on, glancing at a paper in his hand. 'You're going back to . . .' He paused again. He did not want to say, 'That house?'

'Home.' She supplied the word for him. 'I am going home.'

He studied her thoughtfully for a moment, saw the overlying timidity that everyone saw at first, and beneath it the stubborn resolve he had encountered so often in their relationship. She was a very contradictory girl, he thought; she was not all of a piece. He liked patients who could be easily categorized; it made it so much easier to keep files and records, for one thing.

'Well, I only wanted to tell you goodbye,' he said. 'And good luck. And, of course, it goes without saying, if you ever need us, if things get to be too much for you out there . . .'

'Things won't get too much for me,' she said; implicit in her words was, 'I won't be back.'

When she had gone, he sat for a moment more looking at the doorway through which she had gone. Under other circumstances he might have kept her a little longer. He knew that he had not even cracked the surface of the protective armor she wore so well. But a family squabble had developed over her, and from his point of view the crucial thing had been that the money had been tied up, and no one would pay her bill. Villa de Valle was not a charitable institution, after all. There were state institutions for those who could not pay; although God knows the Wrens could afford to pay. It was part of his job here to see that those who stayed, paid.

He marked her file and put it in the basket for the clerk to file under closed.

* * *

It was Robie who had come to pick her up, just as it had been dear, maligned Roberta alone of all the relatives, the aunts and uncles and cousins and acquaintances, who had come to visit her during her confinement. No one had even sent a card: Sorry to hear you are ill. Get better soon.

She blinked coming into the afternoon sunlight, and paused in the parking lot to look back at the pink building. The Ville de Valle was officially a clinic and, as its sign proclaimed, a rest home. In actual practice it was a private mental hospital for those who could afford such discretion, and needed it.

'I won't be coming back here,' she said aloud.

'Of course not, silly,' Robie said. 'Here's the car, honey.'

'I mean it,' Helen said. 'No matter what, I won't be coming back here. I would rather die.'

'Poor Helen,' Robie said. 'I don't blame you. All that awful pink. But you know, if you will get into the car, we can leave faster.'

They had been standing by the car, Robie

waiting patiently. Helen laughed, suddenly feeling very happy, and bent down to open the door.

Robie's car was a vintage Jaguar. The top was down; it was, in fact, nonexistent.

'When it rains,' Robie used to say, 'I just carry an umbrella.'

It was a wonderful sensation to be moving, free like this with no one trying to restrict her. Not that she had actually been an inmate, or Villa de Valle a prison. Her confinement had been more or less voluntary, but she understood well the subtleties of confinement without bars and locks. She had not been free.

Now, for a time, she could even not be frightened by Robie's madcap style of driving. On the expressway, traveling at an electrifying high speed, the wind noise in the open car made conversation difficult if not impossible. Later, when she was negotiating the curves on Wyatt Boulevard with an absentminded ferocity, Robie said, 'I still think you ought to come up to New York for a visit with me. It would give you time to get your legs back, so to speak.'

Helen smiled and made a doomed attempt to push her hair back from her face. The wind whipped it out of her hands and blew it into her eyes again.

'Put off going back to the house, that's what you really mean, isn't it?'

'I shouldn't think you'd be awfully eager to

go back there,' Robie said.

A gray sedan pulled from a side street into their lane. Robie flattened the heel of her hand on the horn button and whipped the Jaguar smartly around the offender.

Helen, who had braced herself stiff-armed against the dashboard, breathed loudly and said, 'I talked it over with the doctors. You know, if I don't go back there now, I will never go. It's like going up in a plane again after a crash. You have to do it right away, before the fear has a chance to set in and take over. Otherwise, you will never get over it.'

'In this case, that might not be such a bad thing. All right, don't go looking all defensive. You know I always say just what I think. But I also stood up for your right to come back to the house unchaperoned, if that was what you truly wanted. Cupcake, you know, don't you, there wasn't exactly unanimous approval among the relatives? About . . . well, about your coming back to the house by yourself, for instance.'

Robie shot a quick glance at her, then back to the street. She slowed for an intersection and turned into a tree-lined street. Large old houses, some of them hidden by the trees, stood back from the street in magnificent isolation from one another, and from the world at large.

Helen managed a smile for Robie's attempt at tact. 'What you're trying to say,' she said, 'is that the general consensus was that I should stay at the happy farm.'

Robie grinned and said, 'There was some talk that way. And it could be made to happen, in case you don't know that. Relatives can have someone put away, permanently. Oh, look, I'm not trying to stir up trouble, damn it, I just want you to understand how the wind blows. If Aunt Willa, for one, were to find a good excuse to send you back, she would. You may as well know that. And she isn't the only one.'

'I know,' Helen said. She reached across and patted Robie's hand on the gear stick.

'That's all the more reason for me to go straight back to the house, don't you see, to keep up an air of normalcy. Anyway, I want to. I want to bury . . . everything that happened.' She nearly added, 'If I can,' and checked herself. Confidence was important just now, even a show of confidence.

'It isn't very nice, is it, having to be wary of your own relatives,' Robie said. 'I mean, you ought to be able to trust family, wouldn't you think?'

'I expect it's father's money. That brings out the worst in people.'

She turned to look at her sister; Robie, with her bleached hair and her mouth painted scarlet, driving an outdated sports car as if she were in a hurry to get to hell. Robie, who had escaped.

Escaped, for God's sake; *as if it were a*

prison, and not her home . . .'

'Robie, did he leave you any money?'

Robie laughed, with surprisingly little bitterness. 'Not a sou. I never expected him to. He told me when I left I'd get nothing unless I came back, and I told him I would never come back, and each of us believed the other meant it.'

She was slowing the car again, turning into a drive. There were wrought-iron gates across it. Helen jumped out to open them, and got back into the car, picking up the conversation as if it had not been interrupted.

'I'm sorry about the money,' she said. 'But you know that anything I've got is yours.'

'I don't need it,' Robie said, emphatically. 'I've got a good job and, this month at least, a good man, and a great little apartment, which I would not for a moment trade for this . . . this thing.'

She indicated with a wave of her hand the house toward which they were driving. It was a large old house, deteriorating from regality into a certain arcane gloominess. Its turrets and cupolas, its gables, its shutters, some of them closed over the windows, gave it an atmosphere peopled with shadows of the long ago past. One felt instinctively that a house this old could never be truly empty.

'The only thing I was ever sorry about was not taking you with me when I went,' Robie added, bringing the car to an abrupt stop in front of the steps leading up to the big front door.

'I was too young. Anyway, it would have killed father,' Helen said, and then flinched at the realization of what she had said.

Robie pretended not to notice. 'No, but he would have killed us. Father is . . .'

'Was,' Helen corrected.

'. . . was a bastard. I'm sorry, I know, respect for the dead and all that. Only my respect died a long time before he did. And it didn't die a natural death, either; he killed it, and I'm not going to pretend otherwise, not even if they threaten me with a stay at that happy farm . . .' oh, Lord, Helen, I'm sorry, that wasn't very nice, was it, you know I didn't mean anything.'

'I know,' Helen said absentmindedly. She was not looking at her sister now; her attention was fixed on the house before them, her gaze riveted on the big paneled door. She had hardly even heard what Robie said, and she did not move now when Robie clambered out her side and started to reach for the bag jammed behind the seats.

Robie finally noticed Helen's lack of motion, and paused, asking, 'Are you all right?'

'Yes,' Helen said. But she remained where she was, her hands clasped in her lap, staring up at the door. After a moment she said, 'This is the first time since it happened, you know. I never came back after that night. They brought the entire jury, and the court reporters, and everyone up here, but I didn't come. The doctors insisted it would be bad for me. Doctor Ida explained it all to me later.'

She let her gaze drift, across the narrow lawn, along the drive; the grass looked freshly cut, although no one had lived here for more than a year; no one had *lived*, that is to say. At the north end of the house was a splash of magenta, the bougainvillea still blooming. A jay, shrilling as he went, flashed across their line of vision. In his wake, everything seemed still and quiet, everything except what was within her.

I think, Doctor, that was the first I knew. No, I didn't know, exactly, but I suspected something. I had a sense of someone waiting, and I thought suddenly that it was the house that was waiting. It was laughing at me, laughing and waiting. The other children in school used to call me Crazy Helen, because I never did any of the things they did. Crazy Helen. All I ever did was hurry home to his house, just as I was doing this time. Any minute, I thought, the front door will open and he will be standing there, looking at me, and then looking at his watch, to see if I am even a minute late.

And then, the door did open. It horrified me, that sudden swinging back of the door. The suddenness of it, the expectedness of it, my imagination—for an awful moment I almost screamed.

'There's Mrs. Halvorsen,' Robie said. A

short, plump woman with a pink face and silver hair appeared in the doorway.

'Mrs. Halvorsen,' Helen said, and got out of the car, coming up the steps with Robie. She was so happy to see a familiar face that she could even imagine she and the housekeeper had been fond of one another in the past, which they had not. She could even overlook the fact that Mrs. Halvorsen did not return her enthusiasm. The older woman standing at the door watched her come up the stairs; she returned Helen's happy smile with a face void of expression.

'Robie told me you'd agreed to come back,' Helen said when they had reached the door where Mrs. Halvorsen was standing. 'I'm so glad. It's nice to see someone I know for a change.'

'I can't come full time,' Mrs. Halvorsen said, stepping aside to let them come into the hall. 'I can come mornings, and all day Thursday if you want me, but I can't come full time, and I won't come evenings. I wouldn't come at all, but Miss Roberta said she couldn't get anybody else to set foot in the place and I thought there should be someone here to help out. I'm sorry, Miss, no offense meant.'

'And none taken,' Helen said with a smile, but she had checked her enthusiasm and the moment had gone a little flat for her. She took a step along the hall and looked about.

'Well,' she said. She knew they were

watching her closely, and trying not to show it. She felt it important that she look unconcerned, but she could not stop the pounding in her chest. She went to the foot of the stairs; she had the impulse to run up them, but at the bottom, with her hand on the bannister, she stopped, looking down at her hand. She was glad her back was to them for a moment, to let her get her breath.

Again she said, 'Well.'

Roberta stirred then, setting the suitcase down loudly on the tile floor.

'I guess he won after all,' she said, looking around also.

Helen took a deep breath, to try to still her trembling, and turned. 'Who?' she asked.

'Father. I said I'd never set foot inside this house again, and here I am. So I guess he won. Are you all right? You look like hell.'

For a moment Helen almost said something. It was like a flood water rising within her, threatening to break over the dam of her restraint. But knowledge reinforced her restraint, the knowledge that Robie alone had championed her sanity, her desire to be released and come home, and that if Robie's confidence in her faltered, she might be going back to that awful pink building. And no matter what, she could not go back there.

She glanced at Mrs. Halvorsen, but the housekeeper's attention was riveted for the moment upon some mote of dust she had spied upon a console.

When they were little, Helen and Robie had played a game; one of them might say, at any time of day or night, 'Freeze,' and the game was that they had to freeze in whatever position they were in at the time, until the other one cried, 'Melt.' And presumably, if the other player never called 'Melt' they were frozen in that position for all eternity.

'We are playing freeze,' Helen said to herself in the seconds in which she hesitated at the foot of the steps. She saw them frozen in eternity just as they were in that moment: Mrs. Halvorsen, bringing the weight of her Scandinavian disapproval down upon an unsuspecting piece of dirt; Robie, fidgeting from one foot to the other, wanting to be gone, to be on her way home to New York, and at the same time wanting to stay, to do her duty; and she herself, trying not to react to the blood on her hands, blood from the bannister, wet and crimson, making her stomach give a warning turn.

'Look, Helen,' Robie said; she came across the hall to stand in front of her sister and clasp her hands. 'I don't have to go back tonight. I mean, it isn't the end of the world if I don't get back. I could telephone Joe, and tell him I was staying over . . .'

Helen gave her head a shake. 'Now don't start fussing over me. I'm all right, really I am. I'm not afraid. And Mrs. Halvorsen will be here if there's any sort of difficulty.'

'I won't work nights,' Mrs. Halvorsen said emphatically. 'Usually I'll be here mornings, but I came this afternoon because you were coming home.'

Helen paid no attention to her. She did not think it mattered in the slightest if Mrs. Halvorsen stayed the night or if she did not. Mrs. Halvorsen, obviously, had not seen the blood, and neither had Robie. And neither, now that she looked down at her hands clasped in Robie's, did she. It was gone, and she had only imagined it, and she could never, never tell them she had seen it, or let them know how it had frightened her.

'Tell you what,' she said aloud, forcing a bright grin. 'I'll take this bag upstairs and we'll have some coffee before you go, all right?'

'Great,' Robie said.

'I'll make some coffee,' Mrs. Halvorsen said, and started in the direction of the kitchen.

Robie looked about to suggest that she come upstairs with Helen, but she did not. She was, after all, the champion of independence and self-assertion. She smiled and nodded and went toward the den. She walked briskly, as she always did.

Helen started up the stairs. She did not hold the bannister, but kept as far from it as possible, leaning against the wall. But she could not keep her eyes from the carved wooden railing nor from the crimson smears upon its polished surface.

Blood. Blood everywhere, up and down the stairs, that dripped from the bannisters onto the stairs themselves, and onto the pale carpeting, and that stained the silk-covered walls with grisly handprints.

CHAPTER TWO

There is a lure to evil, don't you think, doctor? That is to say, intellectually we may be attracted to goodness or virtue. We may even want virtue. But wickedness has a mystique of its own. We read books of violence and we watch shows of violence on television or at the movies, and we tell ourselves that it is the drama that counts, but we are deluding ourselves. It is the violence that counts, the bloodshed and the horror and the murder. We are fascinated by murder. There is some silent well deep within us that flows in rhythm with these currents of evil. We are drawn to the man or woman who we know is evil.

I think I knew from the first that something evil had inhabited that house, and was in possession there. There was an aura of doom about the place; and it was this, perhaps, that added presence, that both frightened and fascinated me.

'Do you think you should? You have a long drive ahead of you.'

Robie, who had gone to the bar to pour herself another drink, laughed and poured without any hesitation.

'Don't worry about that,' she said. 'My car knows the way home by this time. All I have to do is sit and hang on.'

She looked over her shoulder at Helen, sipping her coffee and sitting on the edge of her chair as if she expected something to happen.

'Why don't you have one, too? It would do you good,' she suggested, stretching to get another glass off the shelf.

Helen gave a flustered little laugh and a wave of her hand and said, 'Oh, I couldn't.'

'Why couldn't you? There's no one now to give you orders, you know.'

'Yes.' Helen paused, and then said, 'It's strange, but I miss that. You get used to a thing, you know; a habit is stronger maybe than love. I've missed having him boss me about, coming into a room and telling me what to do and what to wear and what to think. I feel, I don't know, unattached, I guess is the word.'

'You have me,' Robie said, coming to her and bringing her a drink anyway. Helen took it meekly.

'That's awfully little, though, isn't it?' she asked. 'Oh, I don't mean that the way it sounded; of course I love you dearly. But I mean, except for that, there is nothing. I have you, and this house, and nothing else at all. Other people have friends, husbands and wives, children, enemies, even. I have nothing.'

The conversation was morbid and Robie did not feel much inclined to pursue it. 'You have to get out and make friends. It's not as hard as it sounds.' She lifted her glass. 'Here's to being free.'

Helen lifted hers too, and sipped tentatively from it. 'I used to think about being free,' she said, more as if she were thinking aloud than talking to her sister. 'Sometimes I used to think it was because of him that I wasn't.'

'Well, of course it was him,' Robie said. 'He wouldn't let you be.' She dropped into a big chair, propping her feet up on the stool before it, the way her father never used to let her do.

'No, it wasn't him,' Helen said. 'Because if it was, you see, I would have become free when he died, wouldn't I?'

'Well, of course you've been at that—that place,' Robie said.

'I don't think that matters very much. I think bondage or freedom is a condition that exists within the individual, independent of any outside master. I knew people at the Villa de Valle who were quite free. Just as there are people out here who are never free.'

Robie had been looking at her over the rim of her glass. She did not like this sort of conversation. She was fond of her sister, and she felt sorry for her, but both of those emotions were tinged with a certain guilt. She had not been able to free herself of the feeling that, when she had run away and escaped this house and their tyrannical father, she had made things worse for Helen. His anger and his bullying cruelty had all borne down upon the younger child, who had been thirteen at the time. Robie's freedom had been tainted by the thought that she had purchased it at the cost of her sister's enslavement.

She had never discussed this with anyone except her psychiatrist, and she did not therefore welcome conversation along these lines. She finished off her drink neatly and put the glass down with a bang.

'Right,' she said, standing in the sudden leaping way she had. 'Love, I have to hit the road. You're sure you don't want to come with me? Last chance.'

'Quite sure,' Helen said, standing more slowly. She put her own drink aside. She had hardly touched it.

She walked with Robie out to her car. She had an impulse to hold on to Robie, to physically delay her departure, but she resisted it.

'It will be nice to be by myself for a change,' she said aloud, partly to convince Robie and partly for her own reassurance. 'After all that time being watched constantly.'

'I hadn't thought of it that way,' Robie said. 'I guess it will be a relief.'

'Yes, it will,' Helen repeated.

They embraced again at the car, and finally Robie was gone, speeding noisily down the drive and disappearing onto the street. She left the gates standing open, as she always used to do. Helen strolled down the drive to shut them again. As she used to do also.

Coming back, she paused at a distance and surveyed the house. She wondered if she had made a mistake by staying. She could have gone with Robie to the city.

At the thought she wrinkled her nose a little. It was prudish of her, she knew, and yet she had recoiled at the thought when Robie had first suggested it; the idea of sharing an apartment with Robie and a man she was living with, a man she wasn't even married to. She would never have been comfortable.

It was strange even to her that she should have reached womanhood with so many attitudes that she knew were prudish and old-fashioned. Certainly it was a result of her father's repression of her. Yet often she had thought he had been justified in that repression. So many times she had found herself thinking of dirty things, things she knew were wrong for a girl to think. It had seemed to her to support her father's theory that girls were by nature wicked. At least in her sometimes fantasies she knew that she was. She had tried, though, to fight against that part of her nature, to bend herself to his will, and to what she knew to be 'goodness.'

Of course, with maturity had come a certain intellectual freedom. She had learned that women were not by nature necessarily wicked. Intellectually she thought of womanhood as a fine thing, and she even admired the feminists and the liberationists. But she had been early and well indoctrinated into other attitudes, and secretly one part of her continued to be ashamed that she was a woman, from whom all sin could be traced, as her father had put it.

Mrs. Halvorsen had prepared an early dinner for her—a cold meatloaf and some salad and a fruit pie—that was laid for her in the dining room. Evening was approaching and the housekeeper was getting ready to leave for the day. She seemed to be experiencing a certain hesitation in going, however.

'You're planning to stay here by yourself, are you?' she asked, standing by the door, one hand on the knob.

'Yes,' Helen said, and when she saw that the other woman was still hesitating, she said, 'It's all right. I'm not frightened of being here by myself.' It was not altogether true, but she had always regarded complete honesty as a luxury she could ill afford.

'Well, I guess lightning isn't likely to strike the same place twice,' Mrs. Halvorsen said, tugging the door open. 'Good night, then,' she said, and she was gone.

'Good night,' Helen said to the closing door.

Alone in the house, she put off what she knew that eventually she would have to do. Instead, she returned to the dining room and ate the dinner that Mrs. Halvorsen had prepared. It had been a long time since she had eaten anything other than the badly prepared food at the clinic. She supposed this was delicious; Mrs. Halvorsen was an excellent cook. But although she ate slowly, it seemed completely tasteless to her.

She hardly paid any attention to the process of eating. Several times she stopped with her fork lifted halfway from plate to mouth and cocked her head, listening. The silence in the house was complete, excessively so. It was the sort of silence that follows someone holding his breath. The entire house seemed to be doing that, holding itself in. Not a board creaked, not a curtain rustled.

At last she pushed her plate aside and determined that she must forget the ghosts at once, if she was ever to relieve the tension that she had felt mounting steadily within her since her arrival home.

She went to the hall, to the stairs leading up. The bannister was clean now, brightly polished with no trace of blood upon it. How could she ever have imagined otherwise? As if Halvorsen would have allowed any traces of that night to remain visible.

She went up the stairs slowly, her eyes

scanning the steps and the carpet. Every stain was gone; there was nothing to indicate the events that had happened here.

Her own room she had seen earlier in the day, but it had held no terror for her. Nothing had really happened there. It was her parents' rooms that drew her now.

She went to her father's room first. He had not shared his wife's bedroom for many years. 'We want to set an example for the children,' he had told his wife when she questioned the arrangement. Anyway, he was a man of considerable energy, and he often worked through the night at his desk. So the largest of the upstairs rooms had been made into a combination bedroom and study for him. It was the first room to the left at the head of the stairs.

There was a sound as she opened the door, a faint, scurrying sort of noise. She supposed that mice had gotten rather free with the house during its period of disuse. But there was nothing to be seen when she looked in.

When she had last seen the room it had been a grisly sight. Lamps broken, tables overturned, the desk on its side. And across the floor, in a grim trail leading to the hall and down the stairs to the foyer below, had been the crimson stains. Now it had been thoroughly cleaned and straightened around.

Her father had been a big man, and strong. He was over fifty. Four young men, all in their prime, armed with guns and knives, had taken him by surprise; and yet they had barely been a match for him, and before they had felled him, he had broken from the room and nearly made it out the front door, dragging his attackers with him, from all the indications. He had left most of one hand behind in his office, apparently severed at the onset by a blow from a machete. With pieces of finger and flesh and tendon dangling from the stump, he had fought his way to the hall. He had been struck in the back of the head by something, a hammer perhaps, and there were seven bullets in his body. And still he had nearly reached the door. It was as if something supernatural, something more than human, had been within him.

At that, he had saved her life, although that had probably not been his intention. It was the noise of the struggle, the shouting and the crashing of furniture and the shooting, that carried across the wide lawns to the neighboring property where old Mrs. Carston was walking her Pekingese in her garden. It was she who had called the police and they arrived in time to spare Helen what otherwise would surely have been a tragic fate. So it was really her father, who had never truly indicated any affection for her, who had saved her life. She supposed she owed him that.

The police did not arrive in time to save Helen's mother, though. She died between the time her husband died and the police arrived.

Helen left her father's room and went along the hall to the door of the room in which her mother used to sleep, and in which she had died. It was the last room along the hall, its windows overlooking the lawn in back, with its goldfish pond and its hanging willow tree.

She did not open the door at once. She had not been in the room that night, nor since then, nor did she even know what had gone on here. But she knew that it had been horrible.

She could not quite bring herself now to open the door in front of her and go into her mother's bedroom. Something held her back, some primitive fear, although reason told her that any evidence of that night would have been erased from here as it had been elsewhere throughout the house. But she could still not quite bring herself to touch the door.

She stood staring at it, and it seemed to her that she could hear sounds from within—vague, indefinable sounds, like a rustling in the wind, like voices whispering ever so faintly.

What could they be saying, those whispering voices, she asked herself.

She was suddenly aware of a chill. It was freezing in this one spot before the door, though it was a pleasant evening. It seemed as if a cold draft blew just along here. Yet it was not exactly like a draft because the air was not moving. It was as if that damp chill were rising from the floor itself.

She gave a start. Someone was knocking loudly, demanding entrance.

'Now, who . . . ?' she said aloud. It was evening by this time, and since she had come upstairs the house had dwindled into darkness, as if sinking into an abyss.

She went back along the hall, but as she neared the stairs she slowed her steps. The knocking did not come from downstairs after all, but from here, from within her own bedroom.

Robie had gone, and Mrs. Halvorsen, and she ought to have been alone in the house. Yet here was the knocking, coming from within her room. Tap, tap, tap—then a pause, and again, tap, tap, tap.

She opened the door of her room. It was dark within, and the lamps were across the room, one on the nightstand and another on the dresser.

She was afraid to step into that dark room and afraid to ask, 'Who's there?' While she was standing in the doorway, something moved, something blocking for a moment the faint light coming through the window. She almost screamed.

Then her shoulders slumped a little and she let out the breath she had been holding. She went across the dark room to the dresser, turning on the light, and from there went to the window.

Opening it, she leaned out to catch the

shutter that was blowing in the wind, and fastened it back properly. The knocking ceased.

She went back down the stairs to finish her supper.

She felt as if someone were watching her.

CHAPTER THREE

A presence of evil. Perhaps that is what it was that I felt with me in that house. Perhaps it was this that followed me along those shadowy halls, that whispered just out of my range of hearing.

I felt that there was something there, something vague that I could not put my finger on. I did not try to think what it was, nor why it was there, perhaps because I did not want to know. But I felt it, following me; always following me.

At first there was nothing that happened, nothing concrete; nothing except that business with the beds.

* * *

It was not until several nights later that she woke during the night under the lingering influence of a bad dream. It seemed to her as she lay staring up at the ceiling, invisible in the darkness above, that she was not alone in the room. She thought she heard faint noises, she did not know just how to identify them, coming from the other bed in the room.

That bed had been Robie's, and had simply never been moved out when Robie left home. Year in, year out it had remained in exactly the same spot, always neatly made up for the sleeper who never returned to it.

Now, though, Helen would almost have sworn that someone had returned to it. Now that she was actually listening, it sounded to her as if someone was in that bed, sleeping badly, tossing and turning, and breathing heavily.

It gave her a horrible feeling to think that someone was in the room with her—not only in the house, where she had thought she was completely alone, but in the very room, in the bed near her. She felt physically ill, and so stricken with terror that for several long moments she could not move at all, nor scarcely think. She lay as if a monstrous weight pressed down upon her, and her thoughts were like the debris blowing before an autumn wind, chasing here and there, settling nowhere.

At last she knew that she would have to move, would have to see for herself what was in the room. She could not afterward have described what it cost her to summon the strength merely to turn her head, to look in that direction. The curtains were drawn, and there was some light from the waxing moon.

At last she moved, the bed creaking slightly beneath her as she shifted her weight. She looked in the direction of the other bed, and as she did so, something happened, so sudden and so startling that it seemed her heart actually stopped beating.

Someone sat up in her own bed; not in Robie's bed, nearby, but in her own bed, directly beside her.

She gave a terrified little bleat and, rolling and kicking at the bedclothes that seemed like so many fingers strangling her, she half leaped, half fell out of the bed on the other side.

There was a lamp on the dresser and she flew to it, almost knocking it over as she searched for the switch. Her entire body jerked convulsively in the spasm of fear that raced through her as the light came on. Her eyes wide in awful anticipation of what she would see, she turned toward the bed.

But there was nothing there.

Nothing.

She stood, actually clinging to the edge of the dresser with one hand, and let her eyes go around the room, but there was no sign of anyone. And because she could still not quite believe that, she went to the other lamp, casting apprehensive glances over her shoulder as she went, and switched on that light as well.

But the room was really empty, at least so far as the naked eye could see. It occurred to her that, to be sure, there were places someone could hide, and that she ought to look more carefully—under the beds, for instance, and in the closets. But she knew she had not the courage to do that. It took more than she had in her to bend down and lift the bedclothes and look into the darkness beneath her bed.

But neither could she turn out the lights and get back into the bed. She saw now that she had been dreaming and that, as sometimes happens, the dream had lingered into the waking state, so that awakening had occurred with no definite line of comprehension between sleep and wakefulness. She understood that this was the result of the strain she had been under, and her nervousness at returning to the house, and being alone there the past few days. Too, there was her own tendency toward fantasy, which her father had often criticized her for.

But understanding these things did not make it any easier for her to return to her bed just now, let alone risk falling asleep and repeating the experience. She felt as if the dream were lingering in a corner of the room, waiting for her to fall asleep again, so that it could come out to haunt her once more.

She left the lights on and sat in the small slip-covered chair by the dresser. She was gradually aware that the night had turned icy cold, although it had been warm enough when she went to bed. She got up to get herself a blanket from the bed to wrap around her.

In the seconds that she stood by the bed, tugging the blanket free, even while telling herself such fears were absurd, she could not quite get over the frightening possibility a hand might reach out from beneath the bed and grasp her foot. She told herself in no uncertain terms that this was sheer nonsense, but she nonetheless stood well away from the bed, leaning toward it at an awkward angle to get the covering.

It was nearly four o'clock by the clock on the nightstand when she settled back into her chair. She could not have long to wait for dawn; surely it must come by seven. She did not enjoy the thought of a long wait through the night. All of her rationalization had not entirely dispelled the feeling that there was someone else in the room.

Outside a storm had come up rather suddenly; that no doubt explained the icy chill in the room, she thought. The winds howled and whistled and sounded like a horde of phantom riders circling the house, calling in eerie tones to one another. The house replied in creaks and groanings and it was impossible not to think one heard footsteps in the hall outside the door. For a long time she stared hard at the door, expecting it to open.

She tried to close her mind to these sounds, but found that in their place she suffered from an old anxiety: She imagined herself the victim of all sorts of fatal disorders. She would crouch in the chair counting the beats of her heart, convinced that it was going to stop work any moment now. It seemed as if the heartbeats were irregular and growing in force, as if threatening to burst through the protective cage of her ribs. She thought her breathing sounded ragged, and began to perceive some grave defect in her lungs. The reasoning part of her mind insisted this was silly. She had been given a complete physical at Ville de Valle, and she was certain that all of these ailments would disappear with the coming of dawn. But for the present they refused to be put aside.

After a time her pulse slowed to something closer to normal, and some of the frozen tension went out of her shoulders. She did not relax enough to think of drifting off to sleep again, but at least she was no longer in a paroxysm of fear, and she could even chide herself a little for the violence of her reaction to what had been, after all, a very ordinary experience. She had had a bad dream, that was all there was to it.

It was not hard to think how her imagination had fashioned it either. This was how *that* night had begun for her, that fateful night, with the realization that someone was in her room.

It had been no dream that time, but real, and more direct than an imaginary figure sitting up in bed with her. It had come in the form of a hand on her shoulder, shaking her rudely awake. She had thought it was her father, and started to sit up, one hand already reaching for the lamp on the nightstand.

'Father?' she said sleepily.

Her hand was seized in a rough grip before she could switch on the light and a voice, a bass voice she did not know except that it was certainly not her father's, said, 'Don't move.'

She gave a frightened little moan, and huddled back against the headboard, saying nothing. There was a full moon, and the night was very bright, so she could see well. What she saw was a strange man in a flowered sport shirt and with a thick beard, leaning over her bed. She could see, too, the gleam of metal in the moonlight, the blade of a knife he held in front of him. It was a long knife, looking almost like a sword; later, she would learn it was a machete, but for now it was enough to know that it looked horrible.

He gestured toward the empty bed, Robie's bed, and asked, 'Where's she?'

Helen was surprised to discover that she still had a voice and that it sounded remarkably normal.

'That's Robie's bed,' she said. 'My sister. She hasn't lived here in years.'

He grunted something unintelligible and turned on the light himself, keeping the knife directed threateningly toward her. She was blinded at first, blinking her eyes rapidly. As her eyes became accustomed to the light, she watched him go to the closet door and open it.

Did he think Robie was hiding there, she wondered? The thought, oddly, made her giggle.

He whirled about, startled by the sound. She was silent again, watching him with wide eyes. Even without the knife he would have been frightening. There was something about him, a wildness, a savage animal quality. She shrank back under the covers as he came toward her, all the way to the bed. He leaned over her and brought the knife down so that its point just pricked the skin at her throat.

'Don't make a sound,' he said. His eyes caught the light from the lamp and gleamed in an eerie way.

'Wait here,' he said. 'And don't try to leave. I'll be back.'

For a long time after he had gone, stealing noiselessly into the hall, she did not move at all, but took him at his word. She remained exactly as she had been, cringing against the headboard.

Eventually her arms became stiff from the unnatural position and she let herself sit up and finally creep out of the bed. She went on tiptoe to the door and listened, but she heard nothing outside. She had no idea what was going on beyond the door of her room, but she could not bring herself to open the door and see.

She went instead to the window seat. With the full moon it was almost as light as day outside. She could not help remembering all the horror tales she had been so frightened by as a child, tales that linked the full moon with every sort of monster and ghoul. She thought of werewolves and vampires and wraiths. And the old legends had come true. By the light of the full moon she awaited she knew not what horrors.

Afterward, there was much controversy in the papers and in court, little of which reached her, as to why she did not simply open her door and walk out of the house, which she would have been able to do any number of times without interference while the young men were occupied elsewhere. Or, if that required more bravery than she commanded, there was, outside the window by which she sat, a trellis; that this provided a means of escape from the room she certainly knew, as it was this same trellis that Robie used to escape the room in the years before she left the house altogether.

These were questions that were never satisfactorily answered in the newspapers, nor in court, nor even by the doctors at the Ville de Valle, who had probed this very area on more than one occasion. To be sure, there were theories and countertheories. It was generally assumed that fear had rooted her to the spot and clouded her mental faculties. But none of the theories ever quite seemed to explain it.

Helen did have reasons for her inaction, but they were so intimate, and she was so accustomed to repressing certain kinds of thinking, that she herself was only dimly aware of her thoughts at the time, and afterward she gathered them up carefully and shut them away in one of the dark chambers of the mind that she kept locked to intruders.

She was twenty-seven years old, and although she was pretty, she was a virgin. She had never had a sexual experience. She had never had any sort of adventure of her own.

Chronologically, physically, legally, she was an adult woman. But she had never, not once in her life, gone out for an evening without her father's permission. She had never prepared a meal for herself, nor eaten one by herself before she returned from the clinic to this house. She had never picked out a dress of her own, nor ordered what she wanted from a menu. She had never traveled, except for one trip to the city, which was carefully watched over by her father.

In all her life, she had never had the opportunity to make a wrong decision.

Nothing had ever happened to her that had not been planned and dictated by her father.

Nothing until that night.

And so she sat at the window seat, bathed in

silvery moonlight, and she listened to the uproar that began elsewhere, heard the shouts and the crashing of furniture and the shots; and she did nothing.

It was not a question of hating her father, although she was prepared to admit to the doctors afterward that perhaps she did; she did not consciously wish him to lose the fight for his life, any more than she consciously wanted to lose her own life. Nor was it fear that froze her into inaction, although certainly she was frightened.

If she could have brought herself to do it, she would have crossed the room when the fight burst into the hall outside and gone out into the hall, but not to try to escape, nor to try to help her father. It was a simple truth that neither the thought of escape nor the thought of helping her father in the struggle for his life crossed her mind. She was merely a listener, waiting and afraid.

She could never have told anyone of these feelings, so ill-formed and shapeless in her mind that she was hardly aware of them herself.

But there was more to it than that, something so awful, so shame-inspiring that almost at once she had seized it and thrust it forever away from the light of consciousness in her mind.

While her father was being horribly murdered, she had sat and done nothing, and had felt almost no emotion; this flaw in herself, in her behavior, she could face.

But when her mother died, she did feel emotion. She did not know the exact nature of her mother's death, and would probably never know. But she knew that it had been horrible beyond words, horrible beyond her ability to imagine. And here was the worst of it, that while it was happening, while she knew it was happening and that it was horrible, she had been moved, not by pity, nor even by fear, but by resentment; resentment not of her killers, but of her mother, because her death had interfered.

The bearded man and another, a thin, round-shouldered man who never stopped smiling, came into her room. It seemed as if it had been hours since the sounds of the struggle outside, and she had sat waiting and listening to the silence. But it may have been only minutes.

She rose to her feet as the door opened and the two men came into the room. They closed the door and stood just inside the bedroom, the three of them looking at one another across the width of the room, as if waiting for a formal introduction.

Finally, the man with the beard made a gesture with the knife and said simply, but firmly, 'Take off your clothes.'

She did, lifting her nightgown over her head and dropping it to the floor at her feet. She stood naked before them, in the bright light, and shivered despite the night's warmth. She watched their eyes move quickly over her and then again more slowly. The smiling man ran his tongue nervously over his lips.

The man with the beard came to her, across the room, his eyes fastening on her eyes. Her body trembled, and not alone from fear, shaking so violently that she was afraid she would not be able to remain on her feet.

The man stopped before he had reached her, stopped and listened.

She heard it too. It was a woman's voice, not loud at first, but pitched low. It seemed to creep through the silence of the house.

It surprised her. She had thought, without consciously thinking about it, that everyone else was dead, and she could not imagine for a moment who this woman could be, laughing.

It was a funny sort of laugh, almost a chuckle, and it seemed to drift about the house like a ghost, moving disjointedly along the halls and into the room.

The man crossing the room stood where he was, listening, his head cocked. The other man, the one at the door, had ceased smiling at last and was staring at the door as if he expected the ghostly laugh to come through it in some palpable form.

It stopped, so abruptly that the silence seemed to vibrate in the room.

A moment later, it began again. This time it

was a roar of laughter, a high pealing sound of hysteria. You would have thought her mother was drunk, and enjoying some great joke, she laughed with such feeling.

Then, suddenly, there was a yell, and cries.

Once, when Helen had been a little girl, her father had taken her on a tour of a food-processing plant, and she had heard pigs squealing. She had asked her father why they were squealing like that; he had told her matter of factly that they were being killed. She had not slept for nights after that.

These cries were like that, shrill and chilling, and they sounded not quite human.

Again there was silence for a moment; one horrible shriek, and more silence.

It seemed an eternity that they stood there, she and the two men, frozen like figures in a tableau. Her mother's screams had saved her from whatever they had planned to do.

When the silence was broken again, it was to give way to pandemonium. There was a sudden commotion at the front door; the bell rang, and at the same moment someone began to pound on the door.

In the hall, someone Helen could not see cried, 'It's the police.'

As suddenly as it had begun, it was over. The intruders, with angry shouts, ran from her room, thinking only of flight. Two of them escaped, but were captured later. The others were arrested on the spot.

When the police came into her room they found her seated decorously at the window again, wearing her nightgown and a robe. She could not speak, not even to answer their simplest questions. It was decided that she was in shock, and she was taken quickly from the house to a hospital. Later, when Robie had been summoned and had driven down, Helen, apparently still in shock, was taken to the Ville de Valle, where she had remained throughout the period of the trial.

She had never told anyone the details of that night, and in fact her own memory of them was blurred. She remembered coming into the hall with a policeman. From the hall she could see the devastation in her father's room. She could see, too, the trail of carnage that began in that room and went down the stairs, blood marking a grisly path to the vestibule.

They had covered her father's body with a sheet, but at that moment someone chose to uncover it. She found herself staring down at it for a ghastly moment, and in those few seconds she seemed to see the entire struggle reenacted before her eyes, as if on a screen. It seemed to her as if she had been an eyewitness to it. She could not have seen it more clearly in her mind if she had run along with him.

If she were to live a hundred years, she would never forget her father's face as he lay on the floor of the vestibule. Even in death it was expressive of a strength of will and an energy that would hold death at bay as long as possible.

There was something more that was odd about the look on his face. Perhaps he had come so close to the door that he thought escape actually possible. Whatever the reason, when they struck the final blow, his features were frozen in a look of triumph.

It gave the impression that he had faced the angel of death, and stared him down.

CHAPTER FOUR

'Are you all right, Miss?'

It was Mrs. Halvorsen's voice, completely real, outside the bedroom door. It brought Helen awake with a start. She had fallen asleep, curled up in the chair by her dresser.

She looked quickly around the room with wide eyes. But it was really morning, with the autumn sunlight pouring through the window, and there was nothing here to threaten or to frighten.

'Yes, thank you,' she called back, stretching her legs before her. They were stiff from having been curled under her so long. 'I'll be down in a moment.'

She got up and took the blanket back to the bed. She stood by the bed for a moment, looking down at it, at the spot where she had dreamed she saw someone. The sheet looked wrinkled there, but that no doubt she had done herself, tossing and turning in her sleep. She laughed, suddenly giddy with a sense of relief and delight that it was morning.

By the time she had dressed and come downstairs, the coffee was ready. The storm that had come up so suddenly during the night was ended, leaving no trace, and in the crisp light of a new day there was nothing ominous about the house in which, she reminded herself, she had lived nearly all her life.

She felt a bit foolish for her melodramatics of the night before, and in a sense she was glad after all that there was no one sharing the house with her, to see how foolish she had been. Her father had warned her often that her imagination was vivid to the point of being 'wicked.'

Perhaps that was all it had been.

Mrs. Halvorsen came into the kitchen while she was having coffee. She was already armed with cleaning supplies and had obviously been at work in the other room. Her bustling, no-nonsense manner was sufficient in itself to dispel any lingering gloom. Mrs. Halvorsen was of an unusually large scale, and she was energetic, so that she seemed to fill a room.

'You're usually up before this,' the housekeeper greeted her. 'I thought something might have happened to you.'

'I slept late,' Helen said simply. She had no intention of exposing her bad dream to Mrs. Halvorsen's equally vivid imagination. Heaven alone knew what omens she might read into it.

'Will you be having breakfast?'

'I think not,' Helen said. In fact, she did not yet feel at ease with the housekeeper. If she were honest, she really did not feel at ease with herself yet.

'You had a restless night, I see,' Mrs. Halvorsen said. She went to the counter, where the dishes Helen had used the night before were stacked. She began to fill the sink with soapy water.

'Yes, a little,' Helen said, embarrassed that Mrs. Halvorsen had discerned this fact. She would have preferred to leave the subject of the previous night alone, but apparently Mrs. Halvorsen, whose keen eye missed little, had seen that her bed was particularly disarrayed this morning.

'If you'll pardon my saying so,' Mrs. Halvorsen said, without turning from the sink where she was now energetically washing the dishes, 'it's your house and you're welcome to sleep where you like, I'm sure, Miss, but changing beds during the night every night does make a bit of extra work for the housekeeper.'

Helen stared stupidly at the woman's thick back, at the plump hands disappearing and reappearing from the mountain of suds in front of her. She had no idea what Mrs. Halvorsen was talking about.

'Frankly,' Mrs. Halvorsen said, without waiting for a reply, 'I can't think why you would want to sleep in those other rooms anyway. I mean, after the things that happened in them. No offense meant, of course.'

'Yes, I understand that,' Helen said. What she did not understand was Mrs. Halvorsen's remark about beds, and other rooms. Since she had returned, she had slept in her own bed, in her own room, exactly where she should have been sleeping.

She opened her mouth to say so, but Mrs. Halvorsen turned just then to look over her shoulder, her busy hands pausing.

'I hope I haven't offended,' she said. "But if I've got to make up three beds every morning instead of just one as I expected, it's going to cut down on the other work I can do, don't you see? I can't come full time.'

'Yes, I do see,' Helen said. Mrs. Halvorsen, satisfied that the issue had been resolved, went back to her dishwashing.

Helen had intended to ask Mrs. Halvorsen what three beds she had had to make up, but it had occurred to her that would surely sound like an odd question. Obviously, Mrs. Halvorsen had to make up extra beds, and she thought Helen knew about them, that she was responsible for them. Helen did not want to say or do anything that would seem too 'odd.'

So she did not ask about the extra beds, but finished her coffee instead, and even forced herself to linger over another cup. Then she left the housekeeper in the kitchen and made her way slowly, thoughtfully, up the stairs.

The door to her father's room was open, and she was certain it had been closed earlier, but Mrs. Halvorsen would have gone in there to dust. She was not one to skip a room.

Helen went to the far end where the big four-poster bed stood. It was neatly made now, and there was no way for her to tell just from looking at it if it had been made this morning, or months ago. And if it had been made this morning, if Mrs. Halvorsen had found it disturbed, when had it been disturbed? She did not say, not even in her thoughts, 'slept in'; she could not bring herself to envision someone actually sleeping in that bed since her father's death.

It was possible that Mrs. Halvorsen herself had left the bed unmade when she had straightened up the house in preparation for Helen's return from the clinic, and she had not discovered the unfinished task until this morning. Helen herself would certainly not have discovered that this bed was unmade. She had come into this room only once, her first afternoon back, and then just to the door. She did not remember even looking at the bed.

Had it been disturbed then? She had not thought so, obviously, but then she just wasn't sure. She had looked at the front part of the room and had given this part of it only a glance.

She went out, closing the door, and walked slowly along the hall to her mother's room. But again she stopped outside the door. She did not want to enter; however unreasonable that attitude was, she had a definite aversion to going in. And there was really no need for her to do so, she told herself. Let the dead bury the dead, so to speak.

If the bed in her mother's room had been one of those Mrs. Halvorsen had had to make up this morning, the same explanation must apply. She had simply been careless and not made them up when she was putting the house in order before; they had gone unnoticed until this morning, when they had given the appearance, an illusion only, of being freshly disturbed.

It seemed odd that Mrs. Halvorsen, such a particular housekeeper, could have overlooked two unmade beds. But what other explanation could there be? She was alone in the house. No one had come to call, certainly not to stay overnight. Discounting her dream of an intruder, and it had been only a dream, who could there have been to disturb beds? The felt, but unseen and unreal presence of memories from the past?

'Memories do not disturb beds,' she told herself aloud. It seemed as if her voice lingered on the air for a moment after she had spoken.

She shivered suddenly. It *was* cold in this particular spot, just outside the door to her mother's room.

CHAPTER FIVE

Later, when Mrs. Halvorsen was preparing to leave at noontime, Helen asked her about the possibility of full-time work.

'I know you said you couldn't work full time,' Helen said quickly, before Mrs. Halvorsen could answer, 'but I thought if perhaps I made it up so you could stay here—I mean, I would give you a room of your own, or several rooms, so that you wouldn't have to commute. It would make things so much more convenient. And it would work out well for you financially, the extra money, and not having to keep an apartment of your own.'

Mrs. Halvorsen, her purse held before her like a protective shield to ward off blows, stood by the open front door and regarded her employer coolly.

'The best I can do is mornings,' she said firmly. 'And all day on Thursday if you want me then.'

'Yes, I understand that,' Helen said, talking very fast now, 'but I only thought it would save you driving, and it would save expenses. You wouldn't even have to keep an apartment if you didn't want to. I wouldn't charge any rent, and you could have . . .'

'If you're afraid to stay here by yourself, Miss . . .' Mrs. Halvorsen interrupted her.

Helen made her own interruption. 'I'm not afraid, Mrs. Halvorsen, I only . . .'

'. . . you should talk to one of the family. I understand that your Aunt Willa didn't want you to come back here in the first place, and frankly, no offense meant, Miss, but I myself can't see why you would want to either. She . . .'

'I'm not afraid here,' Helen said, much more sharply than she had intended.

Mrs. Halvorsen stopped talking. They stood looking coolly at one another for a long moment. Helen was breathing hard and she realized that she had allowed her composure to slip, something she should not do, especially not with a servant. She managed a laugh and tossed her head in a nonchalant fashion.

'I'm not afraid of this house,' she said, more softly. She made a gesture with her hand to take in the foyer.

'This is my home, for goodness' sake. I hope you won't go around telling people, telling my Aunt Willa, for one, that I'm afraid here. There's no telling what they might think.'

After another moment, in which Mrs. Halvorsen surveyed her sternly, the housekeeper said, 'I can't come full time.'

With that she went out, closing the door after herself with a bang.

The sound of the door closing seemed to echo with finality through the hall. Helen turned her back on the door, peeved with the housekeeper. She had made a perfectly good suggestion. It wasn't as if Mrs. Halvorsen had anyone to hurry home to at night, or in the afternoon. Her husband was dead and her children married and moved away; she lived by herself. They both lived alone.

'Isn't that silly,' Helen said aloud, giving her head a shake. 'Two of us living alone, all that extra nuisance and expense and everything, when she could just as easily share this big old place with me.'

She looked down the hall. With the morning light the house was cheery, but now that the sun had moved overhead the shadows were forming and regrouping in the corners.

Helen's eyes went from one corner to the next, and to the stairs leading up. She gave a forced little laugh.

'Well, if she doesn't take to a sensible suggestion, what can I do,' she said, shrugging her shoulders. She went into the living room.

She tried to read, but she was restless and could not concentrate. Anyway, the reading material in the house was a bit tedious. She made a mental note to purchase some magazines later, and maybe a few romantic novels. Her father would never have permitted her to have them in the house before, although Robie had provided her with a few, carefully smuggled in.

She got up and paced the floor for a moment or so. She caught sight of herself in the mirror over the fireplace and decided that she looked wild-eyed. It was no wonder that Mrs. Halvorsen thought she looked frightened. Her face was pale, her lips a thin line. There were shadows under her eyes, evidence of her poor sleep the night before.

'I certainly don't look like myself,' she said aloud.

Having said that, she began to wonder what herself really looked like. She was too familiar with the features to know what impression they made. She looked hard at her reflection, trying to see what a stranger would see.

It was bland, she thought, grimacing. A bland appearance, with her light-brown hair and her oval face and her pale complexion. She wondered how she would look if she bleached her hair the way Robie did. She had always secretly envied Robie for having done that, although now that she was older she could see that it looked a little cheap.

She came closer to the mantel, still looking into the mirror. She pulled her hair back from her face, and then tried pushing it up for still another effect.

There was a movement in the glass. She let

her hair fall, and brought her hands down to the mantel, grasping it for support.

There was a man on the terrace, outside the French doors. The curtains blurred his appearance, giving him a shadowy look, but he was there; she could see his outline, leaning close as if to try to see into the room through the curtains.

He tried the door handle, rattling it. Had Mrs. Halvorsen left it locked? Surely she had.

She almost laughed at herself for that thought—a simple little bolt, fragile enough that anyone, even a strong child, could force it. It was just such a bolt that had given them a false sense of security in the past, just as one felt safe behind a latched screen in summer, a screen that anyone could tear. Safety, after all, was only another illusion, a psychological thing, something abstract that existed irrespective of safeguards such as latches and bolts. Evil could enter anywhere.

'Anyone home?' The handle on the French doors rattled again. 'Miss Wren? Halvorsen?'

She knew then it was not a prowler, but Mr. Boyd, the gardener and general handyman who had worked for them in the past. Of course, someone had been taking care of the place—the freshly cut lawns, for one thing, should have told her that. And who else would it be but Mr. Boyd? She ought to have known.

She went quickly across the room to unlatch the French doors and swing them open. It was indeed Mr. Boyd outside; it was an indication of her loneliness that she was so glad to see him. She had always thought him ugly and a little frightening in the past. He was a squat, broad figure, and he always wore a tattered jacket and loose, floppy trousers. His face was wrinkled and tanned to the color of old oak, his eyes black and fierce. He wore a battered hat, from which escaped a shock of soot-colored hair. All in all, he was quite forbidding looking, and as a child she had been quite in awe of him. Just now, though, he was an inexpressibly welcome sight.

'Mr. Boyd, hello,' she said, resisting a fleeting urge to embrace him, which he would certainly have resisted anyway.

'So you're here, are you?' he said, with no warmth in either his look or his voice. 'Well, welcome back, I guess. I told Halvorsen, that girl's crazy to come back here.'

He did not wait for her to reply to this remark—and in fact she had no reply to make—but went on without pause to ask, 'I was wondering, did you want me to lay the fire for you? It's getting chilly nights, and your father used to like to have a fire when the nights started cooling off.'

'Yes, that would be nice,' Helen said, trying to excuse his rudeness. 'How kind of you to think of it.'

'Your father used to like it,' he said. He came past her into the room and went to the fireplace, where he moved the screen aside.

'Funny thing, I thought I saw him,' he said, bending down and brushing at the already clean hearth with the back of his hand.

She came to stand behind him and watch the operation. She might have to lay a fire herself some time in the future.

'Saw him?' she said to his back. 'Saw who?'

'Your father. I was cutting the grass just the other day, I was clear down at the far end of the yard, and I happened to turn and look up this way, and I thought I saw him, standing just the way he used to stand, at the back door there, watching me work. He used to think if he didn't watch me, I wouldn't get the work done.'

He chuckled at this thought, and the chuckle was faintly colored with a sense of triumph, since after all he and his work had outlasted their watcher. Straightening, he started toward the open French doors.

Helen, staring open-mouthed at him, said, 'But it couldn't have been him.'

He grunted and gave her a scornful look that told her what he thought of her observation.

'Course it couldn't,' he said, and went out.

She sat in one of the big armchairs by the fireplace and stared after the man. She had never liked him, never. He had always treated her like one of the servants, and if she had not been so afraid of her father she would have complained to him plenty of times about Mr. Boyd. True, none of the servants had ever treated her with any real respect. But Boyd was the worst. At least Halvorsen was polite.

Still, she thought, he did take good care of things. She supposed that was something.

He came back in a moment, bearing an armload of firewood, which he carried to the hearth and put down noisily.

'Mr. Boyd, what did he do?' she asked.

He was starting toward the door again. He stopped and looked at her.

'What did who do?' he asked.

'My—the man you thought was my father.'

'Do? Why, he didn't do anything. He looked at me like your father used to do, and then he turned away and came inside, that's all.'

He went outside again. She jumped up and followed him out to the terrace. There was a large stack of firewood against one wall. She followed him to it, addressing his back while he filled his arms again.

'Who do you think it was?' she asked. 'I mean, if there was someone hanging around, I ought to know, don't you see?'

'Some delivery man, I suppose,' he said. 'Halvorsen had a lot of them in and out for days, getting things ready for you.'

He rose, fixing his beadlike eyes on her briefly and not warmly, as if telling her what he thought of people who put other people to such trouble.

'Takes a lot of work to open up a house like this one after it's been closed for a while. Just as much work to open it for one person as for a whole family. Excuse me, Miss.'

He went past her again and along the terrace. But at the door he stopped and turned back for a minute.

'I had to chase some people away from the gate this morning,' he said.

'What did they want?' she asked, surprised by this news. Even when her father had been alive there had rarely been anyone at the gate.

'They came to stare, I reckon,' he said, and went in. She heard him drop the firewood loudly on the hearth.

She had not thought of that: people coming to stare. But, of course, she was a freak now, that was expected. Before, she had no doubt been a bit of a curiosity, but that was all. Crazy Helen, who never did anything the other girls did.

Now, however, murder had been done, and not just ordinary murder, but horrible, sensational murder. There had been a lurid trial, with much publicity. She had been shielded from most of it at the Villa de Valle, fortunately. She had never known whose idea that was, but newspapers and news magazines had been kept from her during the time of the trial, and the doctors had very strictly supervised all questioning sessions with the police; for that, frankly, she had been grateful.

Nor had it been necessary for her to appear in person at the trial. The testimony necessary from her had all been given in the form of depositions. The doctors had insisted upon it, and after all, her evidence had hardly been necessary to convict the four young men, whose guilt was undeniable.

Because the trial had ruffled so little her existence in the pink vacuum that was the Villa de Valle, she had not credited quite how much stir it would make outside. Robie had at least warned her that there had been some notoriety, but that information had not much disturbed her.

So people had come to stare. She could hardly believe it. She left the terrace, walking across the neatly cut lawn toward the gate.

There was no one there now, but as she stood just inside the gate, one hand upon the wrought iron, a car going by slowed almost to a stop. The people in it were staring, staring at her. The wife, on the opposite side, was leaning clear across her husband, who was driving, to get a better view, and there was an older woman in the back seat who lowered her window so that she could see more clearly.

'Look, it's her,' Helen heard one of the women say in a loud voice.

They did not even seem embarrassed that Helen saw them, or that she stared back. She wanted to look away, but she would not let herself.

The woman in the rear seat said something Helen could not hear, and they all three laughed, and finally the car moved on, picking up speed. She could see them, the women, still turning in their seats to look back at her.

It was more than annoying, it was unnerving. She felt like one of the animals at the zoo, behind her iron barred gate, with people coming by to look at her. She wondered what could be done about it.

What did the animals in the zoo do?

She started toward the house, leaving the drive and walking up through the grove of trees. Most of the leaves had changed and were falling. Everything was turning brown and gray, with its depressing sense of finality. Everything was terminal.

She paused to bend down and pick up some sort of seed pod. Out of this death all about her would come new life. But there was no hope in resurrection, because each life returned as itself; not reborn to a new, higher existence, but locked into the same life, the same situations, the same hopes, the same despairs.

She turned the pod over in her fingers. It was shaped, she thought, like a woman's breast. It was shaped like her own breast.

She crushed it in her fingers, letting the pieces fall to the ground, and went quickly toward the house.

CHAPTER SIX

I had been aware, almost from the first, that I was now alone. I was free, independent of anyone else's rule. And yet it was the most trivial of incidents that brought that fact home to me at last. I was free. I was my own person. Can you think what a revelation that must have been to me?

But, of course, I was not free. Who of us is? I had only exchanged tyrants. Are you free, Doctor? Free to do or say whatever you want, whenever you want, with no fear of the consequences? I think not.

* * *

Someone came to call. She was so surprised to hear the bell at the front door. No one had called from down at the gate to ask if they could come up. The gate, she remembered, had been closed, although it was not locked; it had never been locked in the past, although always kept closed.

'Maybe I should keep it locked,' she thought on her way to answer the door. But again, that was like the bolt on the French windows, only an illusion of safety. If someone really wanted to get in, they would do so. The men who had come here that night had climbed over the wall, although the gate was unlocked and they could have come right in that way if they had only tried.

It was Reverend Ellis at the door, explaining in an embarrassed fashion that he had 'rung the bell and rung the bell down at the gate, and no one answered, so I just came on up.'

'It must be disconnected,' she said. 'I'll ask Mr. Boyd to look at it. Come in, please.'

She took him into what had been her father's library, for this was where he formerly entertained the minister when he called. It was a room with which she was not very familiar, and in which she felt a little uncomfortable. As a girl, and even as a young woman, she had not been permitted to come in here. It had been her father's private preserve.

'Would you like something?' she asked. 'A drink, or some coffee?'

'I'm not a drinking man,' he said sternly; but at once the expression mellowed a little, and he added, 'Your father used to give me a glass of his berry wine, though.'

'Of course,' she said. She found the wine in her father's liquor cabinet, and poured him a small glass of it, not daring to pour any for herself. She sat in a chair facing him, and watched him sip the wine, a smile softening the stern corners of his mouth as he tasted its sweetness and licked his lips.

'It's good to see you back home,' he said, making an unpleasant noise smacking his lips.

He leaned back in his chair, his hand on the table beside it, and his fingers curled gently about the stem of his glass. He was a mild, thin man with a high nose and a bald head.

'I am happy to be home,' she said. She was wondering if he had some particular reason for calling, other than to welcome her home. He acted like a man who had something on his mind, but she could not think what he could possibly want of her.

'You have had a difficult time,' he said; she nodded wordlessly.

'But you must remember, my dear, that afflictions, though they are birds of ill omen, are yet spiritually like the ravens who supplied the prophet. And when they visit the faithful, it may be they come charged with nourishment for the soul.'

She did not know what remark to make. She could not see in what way the experiences of the last year could have nourished her soul, but she did not want to offend him by telling him this. She gave him a pale, noncommittal smile, and watched the purple liquid slosh about as he twirled his glass.

'Your dear father would have wanted you spiritually strengthened by what has happened,' he went on. He, too, following the direction of her gaze, stared at the wine in his glass as if it were suddenly fascinating.

After a moment, in which neither of them spoke, he stirred himself and murmured, 'Your father was a deeply religious man.'

It had always seemed to her that religious scruples were acquired by her father only after he had acquired everything else that he wanted. She had no great quarrel with this. She herself had never acquired any deep faith. What fools people were, she thought, to believe that a wise and powerful God should choose a foolish man such as the one before her to represent him on earth. Even a poor earthbound government would choose a better ambassador.

'And,' Reverend Ellis continued, in the same soft, almost whisper of a voice, 'he was such a pillar of support for our church. In every way. It was not alone the money he gave, although he was generous with that. He was a pillar of moral support as well.'

At once she understood. It was suddenly brought home to her what she had been told some time before, but had only superficially grasped: The money was hers. She was not only free of her father, she was mistress of this house and heiress to her father's wealth.

It was as if someone had struck her, rousing her to consciousness. She said, 'Oh,' very distinctly and sat forward on her chair.

The Reverend, frightened by this abrupt change in her manner, and no doubt thinking he might have somehow offended her, set his drink down loudly on the little table and leaned forward so that the two of them looked as though they were putting their heads together to share some grave secret.

To his relief, however, she quickly recovered herself. She smiled, rather brightly this time, and said sweetly, 'Of course, I shall want to continue his support. In every way.'

With this news, the Reverend grew noticeably happier. Again he picked up his glass of wine, this time draining it.

'I know that you are still fatigued,' he said, rising. 'I don't want to tire you. I only wanted to welcome you home, you know, and assure you that I am close at hand, if there is anything you need me for. And of course there is a friend even closer at hand.'

She had been drifting away from him again, into her own thoughts, but she brought herself back and absentmindedly asked, 'And who is that?'

The Reverend looked a little offended that the subtlety of his remark had missed her, but he only said, 'Our Good Lord, of course.'

'Of course,' she said, embarrassed. She had not meant to seem so obtuse.

When they had come into the hall, she paused with him.

'Do you think, Reverend,' she asked, peering into his kindly if not very intelligent face, 'that there may be something that lingers behind when people—when they die?'

'Something that lingers?' he asked, looking puzzled.

'Not of the flesh, I mean. Spirit.'

He brightened and nodded. 'Oh yes, quite. The spirit is immortal, don't forget. Spirits are about us at all times. The flesh profiteth nothing. Just think, that when you imagine yourself alone and wrapped in darkness, you stand as it were in the center of a theater. That was the message of Swedenborg, as I recall, and not without its merits.'

He started toward the door, pleased with his remarks, but he stopped again to carry his point further.

'A theater as wide as the starry floor of heaven, and an audience no man can number, looking upon you as if under a flood of light. So when it seems your body is in solitude and in darkness, remember that you are in light, and surrounded by witnesses. On the other hand, he that loveth corruption shall have enough thereof. Good day, my dear. I shall come to see you soon again, when you are feeling more yourself, and we shall discuss your role in the church. Give my blessings to your dear sister.'

When he was gone, she let herself reflect for a moment upon his remarks. His puzzling philosophy was overshadowed, however, by the realization that she was an heiress. She could not think why that news had had no such impact before. For the first time she truly grasped the fact that she was dependent upon no one, for anything.

On the heels of these thoughts came another. The other relatives had gotten only token inheritances; this, of course, explained why they were so cool, even antagonistic to her. Robie, who had gotten nothing at all, was the only exception.

And this only underlined the truth she had already discerned, and that Robie had warned her of, too. The relatives would have preferred to have her committed, not just to the Villa de Valle, but to an honest-to-goodness asylum. That would give them full control of the money.

Given any opportunity, they would still do so. In reality then she was no more free or independent than she had been; now she was dependent upon her relatives for her freedom. Even more than before, she must guard her every action and word, lest she give them any ammunition to use against her.

She had known all this before, but it had only just come home to her with the Reverend's visit.

She thought of her father and his connection with the church. He had come late, and fervently, to a harsh brand of religion, with principles that would have pleased Calvin or Knox.

'I won't have you doing the kind of things other kids do,' he had often told Helen. That promise certainly he had kept.

But while he eschewed certain things,

drinking for instance, his prohibitions were meant mainly for others, as if he and God determined between them what was good and what was evil. Indeed, he often spoke as if he and that deity were in the habit of discussing things after dinner, over a good cigar. His religious fervor left no doubt that he regarded God as king; but he made it equally clear that he thought of himself as the power behind the throne.

In the evil that followed, God had presumably failed to follow orders.

It was late afternoon. Already the shadows were thickening and concentrating. She went into the kitchen; Mrs. Halvorsen had left some cold roast beef in the refrigerator, so she made herself a sandwich and drank some milk with it, to suffice for her dinner.

By this time it was evening, and she had to turn on lights as she came back to the front of the house to the living room. She decided, as she went, that she would spend some of her newly acquired wealth on rewiring this house; it was old, and the wiring nearly equaled it in antiquation. By evening there was scarcely a corner that didn't remain dark despite all the lamps. The entire house was dim and gloomy. She thought she would investigate fluorescent lighting, perhaps the kind that was concealed in the ceilings, like they had at the Ville de Valle.

She lit the fire that Mr. Boyd had laid. A

sense of gloom had descended upon her unaccountably, and she thought the fire would be cheering.

But it was not. The dancing flames only made the shadows in the corners of the room seem to come to life. She could almost see them, out of the corner of her eye, moving, taking shape. Time and again she turned her head quickly, seeking the source of some motion that had distracted her. But there was nothing. The room was empty yet it seemed to her quite crowded.

She thought of the words of Reverend Ellis, of spirits about her all the time, watching, as in a theater. She had thought these expressions silly, but now they gained a new importance for her. She seemed literally to sense the presence of spirits, surrounding her, observing her every action.

When she rose and went to the kitchen for another glass of milk, she thought she could almost hear the sound of others going before her. It was disconcerting and unnerving, and she found herself increasingly on edge.

Suddenly, as she was passing through the dining room, there was another body. Another face equally startled, equally afraid.

It was only her reflection, though, in the mirrors. There were mirrors on each of the walls, so that as she paused and looked about, she found herself surrounded by watching strangers who proved to be only images of herself. Their eyes watched as she flew by them and into the kitchen.

They were still watching when she came back, and each one she glanced at was glancing at her.

She was almost happy to be back among the shadows before the fireplace.

* * *

I hardly know how to describe what I felt during that period. It was like a dream in which you see a face you know, but cannot identify; and the face is smiling and in every way cheerful, and yet you feel frightened by it, and you do not know why. And you awaken from the dream, knowing that you were frightened, and with the fear lingering, but you do not know why you were frightened, what produced the fear.

That was how I felt now. This was my home. I knew each of those shadows intimately. I was acquainted with every creak and groan of floorboard or rafter. I could have given each rustle of curtains in the breeze a name, and called them by that name thereafter.

And yet I was frightened, and did not know what it was that frightened me.

Have you ever felt that, Doctor? Have you ever looked at someone you knew, a friend, or a loved one, and seen, for a fraction of a second, something new and frightening, something you could not even name, but that gave you a chill?

Have you thought, ever so fleetingly, that they hated you, that they would harm you? Has a familiar room ever suddenly struck you with reasonless terror? Has something dull and commonplace ever inexplicably caused your blood to run cold?

That was what I felt in that house.

* * *

At last she felt she could tolerate no more, and although it was early she put the screen before the fireplace and made her way upstairs. It seemed when she was in her own room that it had gotten colder.

When she was in her bed, in the dark, all of her earlier tension and uncertainties combined to assail her. She tried to close her mind to all thought, she drifted close to the brink of sleep—and then would start at some little sound and sit up clutching the bedclothes. Reasoning did no good then; all the logic in the world could not still her racing heart or restore her labored breathing to normal.

She concentrated her thoughts upon harmless things, gentle things. She counted daisies and sheep, and recited old poems. But when she started to recite 'How Do I Love Thee,' her thoughts drifted to the lurid memory of an auto crash she had seen as a child. A car tearing through the intersection, around and past her father's car, had been rammed by another crossing vehicle.

She had watched from the back seat of her father's car as the struck vehicle spun around and around and around; she had seen through spinning glass the faces inside, faces distorted by terror. Until it collided into the telephone pole, even with enough power to set it at an absurd angle. And for a moment, all motion had ceased.

Her father, not wanting to be made a witness, had turned and driven away from the scene, ordering Helen and Robie to close their eyes. But when Helen had closed hers, the scene had replayed itself over and over again in her mind. It came back to her now, vivid in its details.

These and similar thoughts worked upon her until she felt that she could cry with frustration and tension. She was in agony. And finally, when she despaired of ever sleeping, and was just deciding that she might as well get up and look for something interesting to read, she fell asleep.

This was no gentle restorative sleep, however; she was as haunted asleep as she had been awake, by phantoms that whispered and lurked and leered. She seemed to relive every unpleasant experience of childhood. She was a little girl, with all the terrors childhood is prey to. Every nightmare newly returned.

It was almost with a sense of relief that she felt her father's hand on her shoulder, shaking her awake. She would be glad to escape her tortured sleep, however early it was.

And it was early, because she could tell that her room was still dark, brightened only by the light of the increasing moon.

She opened one eye a slit, and wondered why her father should be rousing her at such an hour. He had stopped shaking her, yet she could still feel the weight and warmth of his hand on her shoulder.

She turned over on her back, and as she did so, the realization hit her like a slap on the face. Her father was dead. It could not have been his hand.

But her room was empty.

She sat up in bed, shaking convulsively and half crying, but there was really no one to be seen in the room with her. For a full moment she waited, expecting someone to emerge from the shadows in the far corner there, by the closet.

No one stirred. The house was as still as if it were holding its breath along with her.

Her mind went back to that other night, to the hand that had shaken her awake. It was the worst nightmare of all, reliving that night of horror.

Finally, still trembling, she stumbled out of bed, and turned on both lights. She grabbed a robe from the closet, not even daring to look into its dark reaches, left her room, and headed downstairs.

She passed swiftly by her father's room. The door was open, the room dark. But she didn't stop to glance inside, for she feared what she might find. She continued downstairs, turning on each light she came to.

She went to the kitchen. The lights there were the brightest in the house; their harsh glare hurt her eyes, but it had a sobering effect. She put on water for tea and brewed a full pot, strong and dark and faintly bitter on the tongue.

She had shut and bolted the old-fashioned kitchen door as she came into the room, and she checked as well the lock on the door that led outside, making certain that it was secured.

She spent the rest of the night there, seated at the maple table in the brightly lighted kitchen. Once or twice she thought she heard steps in the hall outside, and once it seemed to her that there was someone just beyond the door, breathing. She stared at the knob, expecting it to turn.

But it did not, and no one came in until morning, when she heard Mrs. Halvorsen's altogether real and heavy tread, and hurriedly went to slip back the bolt so the housekeeper would not wonder why she had locked herself in the kitchen.

CHAPTER SEVEN

It was a gray morning. It had begun to rain, gently at first and then with surprising intensity. It sounded to Helen like someone tapping at the glass, and the wind, rushing about the corners of the house, was a voice of warning, whose words she could not quite distinguish.

She felt that she must get out of the house, rain or no rain. She could not bear even Mrs. Halvorsen's desultory conversation, and the familiar walls closed in upon her at every turning.

'It's an ugly day out,' Mrs. Halvorsen said when she saw her getting ready to go out.

'I don't mind,' Helen said, putting a scarf over her hair. 'I haven't had much opportunity to get out the last year. It will be a nice feeling to have some rain in my face.'

She did not add that she thought it was less ugly outside than it was in. The house seemed to be mocking her. Every shadow, and there were many on so gloomy a day, seemed to dance and writhe, and subside into stillness just when she looked its way.

It was a relief to be outside. She did not mind the cold wind pushing against her, as if it conspired with the house to keep her there, nor did she object to the cold rain that drove at her. These elements only served to heighten her consciousness and brush away, as it were, the lingering cobwebs of the night's anxiety.

It was only about two miles to her destination. On the way she went past a flower shop and stopped to buy a large bouquet of mixed flowers which she carried cradled in her arms.

The cemetery in which her parents were buried was an old one, the first in the area. At one time it must have stood by itself outside the town, but now housing developments and shops virtually surrounded it, and there was a little cafe across the street from the cemetery's entrance that, with its gaudy signs, seemed especially incongruous.

She went directly to the place where her parents rested side by side. Doctor Ida himself, of the Villa de Valle, had accompanied her to the funeral, and a corps of personnel from the clinic had been on hand to keep the curious bypassers and newspaper people at a distance. The rates at the clinic had been high enough to provide that sort of personal attention.

They had been buried in the afternoon, under the shadow of the gray and antiquated tower of the church. It had been a dreary winter day, and the sky heavy with snow which began to fall during the graveside ceremonies. The coffins were put down by their waiting graves side by side. A few big flakes of snow fell upon them. Helen had been mesmerized by the contrast of white against the black of the coffins.

There had been some hitch in lowering the coffin in which her father lay; something was wrong with the mechanism that performed the task. There followed a hurried discussion among mourners and funeral directors as to whether someone should be brought in to repair the mechanism so that the coffin could be lowered beneath the surface of the ground, as was the custom, or whether it should be allowed to remain where it was for the remainder of the services.

The others of the family had been all for finishing up the ceremonies as quickly as possible, but Helen had decided the mechanism must be repaired, and the coffin lowered. She had offered no explanation for her opinion, but she had been adamant in the face of all argument and cajoling, and at last the others had been forced to give in.

It had not been merely a matter of stubbornness on her part. It had seemed fallacious for her father's remains to linger aboveground. It was as if he still struggled against this, his final assailant, death, and would not be over and put away. Helen could not bear to leave the contest undecided, and it was for this reason that she had refused to continue with the ceremonies until the trouble was corrected.

The funeral party had drawn back from the

site and waited in silence. They rubbed their hands and stamped their feet, pretending not to notice the workmen handling the coffin in such a matter-of-fact way.

Helen spoke to no one while this was going on, but silently watched the big flakes of snow fall gently one by one, like heavenly benedictions, to melt in tears upon the twin coffins. She could not remember, in life, her parents ever having remained so close to one another for so long a time.

When the funeral was done, and she was back in the pink-walled room at the clinic, she had not felt satisfied. She was where she was, and her father was where he was, and yet she could not help feeling that they were not separated. More than once she had come close to asking Doctor Ida for permission to return to the cemetery, so that she could reassure herself that the grave was undisturbed, and her father still there.

She had not dared to do that, though. There was much that she did not dare to do, because the suspicion in which she was held colored everything that she said and did.

* * *

Because once they think that you might be crazy, they never stop watching you and weighing you. And you can't ever be normal again, because that would be unacceptable to them. Normal people act crazy, don't you see? Normal people can do irrational things: lose their temper, or be frightened, or act out of spite, or swear at someone. Normal people can spill drinks on their laps, or forget a name or a word. They can get confused, or change their minds a hundred times, or decide they don't want to eat something they just don't like, or have a hunger for something they didn't like before. A normal person can get angry and throw a book at the wall, or think they hear someone at night, or a hundred other things. Because when you are labeled normal, your actions are taken for normal. But if they think you're crazy, you can't do anything that isn't regarded as a symptom.

* * *

She did not know how long she had been standing by the graves of her parents before she became aware that someone was watching her. For a horrible moment she thought it was the spirits of her dead parents.

But someone made a sound, and looking around she saw a caretaker working at a gravesite nearby; he glanced at her a little curiously, probably wondering why she should be here on a day like this, standing for so long in the drizzling rain.

She divided up the assorted flowers she had brought with her. The pale blue flowers, whose name she did not know, she put on her mother's grave, and the big, bold daisies she laid on her father's. But she had brought roses, too, warm and vibrant, and she did not know what to do with them. Their velvety feel, their color, were too sensuous for either plot, and in the end she took them with her. Still holding them in her hand, she left the cemetery and started home.

Because of the weather there were not many people out. She did pass by three or four women at different times who all seemed to stare at her from under their umbrellas. She knew that she must look queer, out in the rain like this, carrying roses, and with no umbrella. Her scarf was soaked by now, and was dripping water steadily upon her shoulders.

But for all that the women looked at her, she did not think they saw her. She might have been invisible. Hers was the invisibility of alienation and anomaly and the total isolation of people from one another.

She reached the walls that surrounded her home and thought about how these walls had not held out the men who had come to kill. Walls could be climbed easily. Most walls, that is. Today she had passed within inches of other people, yet something seemingly insurmountable had separated her from them, something that could not be crossed. It was a ghost wall. Was it a wall within her, or within them? She did not know.

She was conscious of a sense of inferiority

to other people. She lived in terrifying isolation. All her life she had dreamed of being friends with other people, but she knew there was an unbridgeable gap between her aspirations and the possibilities of achieving them.

When she came to the gates, she looked up and saw the house in the distance. She paused, staring at it through the rain and mist.

She asked silently, What do you want of me? I know you are there. I feel your presence, always on hand, watching, waiting. But for what? Why won't you be done with me? If only I could climb that wall.

She knew that there was a pattern to it all, but she could not perceive its outline. She felt as if she were being drawn into a vortex, sucked inexorably inward and downward to a fate she could not perceive.

CHAPTER EIGHT

She came up the driveway, to discover a car parked in front of the house. She recognized it at once as her Aunt Willa's car, a luxurious foreign make.

Helen did not go in by the front door, but instead went around the terrace and in through the French doors. She wanted to put off meeting her aunt, not only because she had been walking in the rain and looked frightful, but also simply because her aunt frightened her. She did not delude herself that this visit indicated any affectionate concern on her aunt's part. Aunt Willa would rather have seen her certified insane and committed to an asylum.

If the truth were known, Aunt Willa would probably have liked to see her dead.

The living room was empty; there was no sign of her aunt or Mrs. Halvorsen. Helen took off her wet coat and scarf, draping them across the back of a chair so that they would drip on the hearth and not on the carpet. She was still carrying her roses; they looked refreshed by the rain and even here in this house their vibrant warmth jarred.

There was a vase on the mantle. She took it down and put the roses in it, setting it on a table.

The hall was empty as well, and she stole quickly up the stairs. In her own room she changed into a dry skirt and sweater and brushed out her hair a little. There was not much point in trying to make herself look glamorous, but she needn't look like a drowned rat, either.

She shuddered at the thought of her aunt's thoroughly aggressive chic; she had always known herself to be mousy in contrast to that. It was difficult for a woman to stand up to another woman she knew to be more attractive than herself, or at least to do so without resorting to a chip-on-the-shoulder sort of defiance. People thought that men were mostly affected by the beauty of a woman, but that was not true. A man might respond to a perfectly plain woman, or even a homely one who exuded some earthy appeal. But a woman never failed to react strongly to beauty, either for or against.

Aunt Willa was just coming along the hall when Helen came down the stairs.

'Good Heavens, there you are,' Aunt Willa said. 'When did you come in?'

'A little while ago,' Helen said. She paused on the stairs, looking down at the elegantly lovely woman who was her aunt. She was wearing a pants suit that might have looked severe on anyone else but on her managed to seem the epitome of femininity. Her hair, this time, was a silvery brown. She was tall and slim, and everything she did, she did with grace. Helen had no idea how old Aunt Willa was. Robie had once said of her, 'She sheds years as easily as she sheds husbands.' And she had shed several of the latter.

'I didn't hear you come in.'

'I was wet,' Helen said. 'I came in by the terrace and went straight up to change.'

'Yes, I see,' Aunt Willa said. The tone of her voice, and the sweeping glance she gave, indicated she did not think things had been much improved.

After a moment she said, 'Well, I've come down for the night. I have to get back to Philadelphia tomorrow. I just wanted to see how you were. We are family, after all.'

'Yes, I know. I'm fine, truly. I was really fine most of the time that I was at . . . that I was away.'

She meant it to be a barb. Aunt Willa had not seen fit to visit her once while she was at the clinic, nor even to write. This sudden interest in her well-being was more than a little transparent.

As if reading her thoughts, Aunt Willa said, 'I wanted to come see you while you were there, but things came up. You have no idea how much trouble can be involved in getting a divorce. You'd think by now I'd have it down pat, wouldn't you? I mean, practice makes perfect, they say.'

She laughed lightly, but seeing that Helen did not get the point, or was not amused, she let her smile fade.

'Are you going to stand there on the stairs all afternoon just staring at me?' she asked a bit peevishly.

'I'm sorry. It's just . . .' She did not know how to finish the statement, and left it to hang in the air. 'Have you had lunch?'

'Halvorsen's just fixing some. I was just going to make a martini. I'm so glad you're here; now I won't have to drink alone.'

She led the way into the living room, as if it

were she who lived there, and Helen her guest. Helen, intimidated, followed meekly after her.

'Good God, who put these roses here?' Aunt Willa asked. 'They weren't here when I came in before, I'm certain.'

'I did,' Helen said. She went directly to her coat and scarf, and decided they were dry enough to put in the closet. 'I got them for the cemetery but they didn't seem right there, so I brought them home.'

Aunt Willa laughed again, a little drily, and said, 'I can't think what made you decide they'd be right here, either. I mean, dead roses? Really, Helen, it seems rather morbid.'

'Dead . . .' Helen stopped on her way to the hall and looked.

The roses certainly were dead. To look at them she would have thought that they were a week old. The stems had gone limp and the blossoms, what was left of them, drooped down the side of the vase. Petals had fallen upon the table and spilled onto the floor.

'They looked so fresh,' Helen said, and then realizing her aunt was staring at her, added quickly, 'I expect they needed water. I forgot to put any in the vase.'

'Oh well, it's nothing to get upset about,' Aunt Willa said. 'A few dead roses.'

'I'm not upset,' Helen said.

'I'm sure it's not good for you to let yourself get all worked up.' She went to the liquor cabinet and began to mix drinks.

‘I’m not upset,’ Helen said again, emphatically.

Aunt Willa paused in measuring gin. ‘Darling,’ she said, without turning, ‘why are you just standing there with those clothes in your arms?’

It is no use, Helen thought as she carried her rainclothes into the hall. I cannot communicate with her on her level. What is normal for her will never be normal for me. But does that make me crazy? My father used to say that she was out of her mind, but I suppose no one ever tried to lock her up.

Her aunt gave her a drink when she came back. ‘Now,’ she said, seating herself regally in the chair that had been Helen’s father’s, ‘let’s have a real look at you. You look drawn, dear. Were you comfortable at the clinic?’

‘Yes,’ Helen said.

Aunt Willa waited expectantly for her to elaborate. The pause grew awkward.

‘I see,’ she said finally. ‘Well, it was certainly expensive enough. I told Robie I couldn’t think how any place could justify that sort of expense.’

Helen wanted to say, But it is my money. She did not. She sipped her drink. It had a bitter, medicinal taste, which she did not like, but the thought of the women in romantic novels who sipped martinis and became involved in romantic adventures came into her head.

The thought did nothing to improve the flavor.

The conversation sputtered, faltered, started up again. Aunt Willa tried a variety of subjects, but the simple truth was that her interests were far removed from Helen's.

Her niece knew nothing of the latest society column gossip, and less about the newest fashion trends. She had never seen a Broadway show, and had never dined in the fashionable restaurants around the world about which Willa loved to reminisce. It was impossible to discuss romance, even on a general level, with a girl who had obviously never been involved.

There was simply nothing of importance that Willa could think of to bring up with Helen, and she found herself reflecting again upon what a peculiar girl her niece was.

CHAPTER NINE

It was an uncomfortable afternoon and evening for both of them; there was no other way to put it. It would have been difficult under any circumstances for these two to share company. Helen could not escape the feeling—no, the conviction—that she was being weighed in the balance. Worse, she very much feared she was found wanting.

Even Mrs. Halvorsen, who, until now, she had reguarded as an ally, however reluctant, seemed to side with her aunt against her. More than once she thought she saw them exchange glances that were charged with meaning.

She knew that they had been alone in the house while she was out. It was obvious that they must have discussed her. Aunt Willa, whose visit after all could only have one purpose, must have questioned the housekeeper about Helen's behavior. Helen could well imagine the sort of things Mrs. Halvorsen had to say.

'She changes beds during the night. I come in and find the beds mussed up in the other rooms. And I don't care what she says, she's afraid of staying here by herself. She tried to get me to change my mind and stay nights. I told her that wasn't the arrangement. I can't come full time, and I won't stay nights.'

She could almost hear these and other charges delivered in Mrs. Halvorsen's emphatic voice. For the first time she began to think that she might be under Mrs. Halvorsen's critical scrutiny as well as that of Aunt Willa's.

Once, during the afternoon, her aunt went to the kitchen on some errand. Helen, who had been pretending to read, found herself staring at the hallway, wondering what had taken her to the kitchen. In her mind's eye she could see her aunt and Mrs. Halvorsen again talking together, comparing notes about her.

'You can see for yourself she just doesn't act right,' she imagined Mrs. Halvorsen saying. 'I ask you, is she like anyone else you know?'

'She doesn't know anything at all about anything going on in the world. I'll bet she doesn't even look at the society page.'

What are they saying? she wondered again and again. What could they be talking about but her? What else did the two of them have to talk about? Aunt Willa would be leaving the next day. It was her first visit in years, and might well be her last for several years more, so she certainly had no pressing need to confer with the housekeeper regarding the schedule of household chores.

The minutes dragged by, and with each passing minute Helen's annoyance and frustration grew. It was not right that she should be spied upon like this in her own home. And it was her home; Aunt Willa was only a guest. If she liked, she could go out to the kitchen now and ask her aunt to leave, and she would be perfectly within her rights. Anyone could see that, even in a court of law.

At last she threw aside the magazine she had been reading and went into the hall, striding along toward the kitchen. But when she came to the dining room, she slowed her pace, and at last stopped altogether at the kitchen door.

Beyond, in the kitchen, she could hear the

murmur of voices kept low—wouldn't they be? She strained to hear, and even put her ear to the door. If only they would speak up, or the door were not so thick. She could do no better than to distinguish an occasional word, not enough to make sense of their conversation.

It made her angry, to be forced into this posture of listening, of spying upon her aunt and her housekeeper to learn if they were spying upon her. She felt like going into the kitchen right then and telling them both what she thought of this whole business.

Instead, she got down on her knees to try to listen at the keyhole. It helped very little. She heard her aunt say . . . can't eat butter . . .' which seemed to be particularly cryptic, since Helen herself had no problem with butter.

She had to know. She had to know what they were planning if she was going to outsmart them. That was her one advantage, that they did not know she was on to them, that she knew they were plotting against her.

If only she could hear what they were saying.

Halvorsen was such a fool to side with Aunt Willa against her like this. What would Aunt Willa do for her? What had she ever done for anyone, except cause them a lot of trouble?

And you, she thought, addressing herself silently to her aunt; it should have been you here that night. It should have been you they hacked with the knives, and beat, and shot. We should have had your rich blood spilled along the hall and down the stairway. And if you try to take me away from here, put me in an asylum, we may, dear aunt . . . we may . . .

'What on earth . . . Helen?'

Helen sat stunned on the dining-room floor, knocked down by the sudden swing of the door. Aunt Willa stood in the doorway, one hand still on the door, staring down at her in bewilderment.

'What on earth were you doing on your hands and knees in front of the door?' she asked.

Helen felt dazed. She gave her head a shake and said, falteringly, 'I—I was looking for something.'

The truth was, she did not know what she was doing in front of the door on her hands and knees. She vaguely remembered coming here, but it was like something she remembered from a long, long time ago, or like something she had done in a dream. Her head hurt, and there was something hovering just beyond consciousness in her mind, like a name that is on the tip of the tongue, but cannot quite be recalled.

CHAPTER TEN

Did you know, Doctor, that I had read Schopenhauer? There was no Raggedy Ann and no fairy tales in our library, and I had to read what was there, or nothing at all.

Schopenhauer says that the will is not free, neither in the stone nor in the philosopher, although both believe that it is. The stone that has been tossed thinks, as it flies through the air, that its will is free, but that is only an illusion. Everyone thinks that he is free in his individual actions, that he can change his life any minute and begin another one, or become another person altogether at any time.

But for all that a man thinks about change, he does not change. He is directed by some necessity, often unknown to him, and from beginning to end he acts out the role that is assigned to him. We do not direct will. Will is the hand that throws the stone; it directs us. We are directed and imprisoned by a life that is a hell. No, worse than hell. How did Dante create his hell, after all? He took all the material from the world of man. There was such a wealth to choose from, wasn't there?

* * *

It was the full moon. She thought of that when

she went up to bed, and for a moment or so she stood at the window looking at the silver-painted world outside, remembering that it was just like this, a night of the full moon, when it had all happened.

She wondered if there were some force at work that had brought her aunt on just this night to stay overnight. Aunt Willa, who had asked, 'Wouldn't you sleep more easily if I slept in the other bed in your room?'

'No, Aunt Willa, I'm quite accustomed to sleeping alone,' she had answered, and thought, They do not give you a nighttime nanny at the Villa de Valle, Aunt Willa. And anyway, I wouldn't sleep at all, thinking all night that you were lying there watching me, watching to see . . . what did she expect to see anyway? Sleep-walking? Some midnight ritual that could be cited as evidence of lunacy?

Lunacy. Luna. From the word for moon. Perhaps they were right, those ancients, to blame the moon for madness. In bed, she fell asleep with these thoughts rambling through her mind.

She did not know just when she ceased to be asleep and dreaming, and when she knew that she was awake and listening to something that was real and not merely a part of her dreams.

But she did not want to be awake. She did not want to know that she was actually hearing it, that low laughing sound that should have been confined to dreams—to nightmares, actually.

It was a woman's voice laughing, almost chuckling. It seemed to creep through the house like a ghost, moving disjointedly along the halls and into her bedroom.

She had heard it before, just like this, sliding into her room under the closed door, rolling and tumbling into the corner by the dresser and back out again, gliding across the floor, rippling across her bed.

'Oh, God,' she thought. 'Oh, God, God, God. Don't let it be what I think it is.'

It was no use praying, though, because she knew without ever a question that it was just what she thought it was: It was her mother's voice. It was the same laughing she had heard the night her mother died.

She knew just when it was going to stop. She could anticipate that horrible silence. She sat in bed, shivering and listening.

It came back a roar of laughter that seemed to make the windows rattle, that filled the room and wrapped itself about her until she could almost feel its touch on her naked shoulders, like little fingers fluttering along her spine.

Stop it, stop it, she cried silently. Go away, for God's sake, go away.

It went on, high and shrieking, hysterical. It was more than flesh and blood could bear, to sit in the darkness and go through all that again. She couldn't even pray anymore, because she knew that if there were a God, he could never, never let anyone go through this, not a second time.

The voice went from laughter to screams, horrible piercing cries and shouts.

What are they doing to her? What have they been doing to her? Oh, Lord, stop it, stop it. I can't stand any more. In another moment I shall go stark raving mad.

It did stop then. For a moment there was that silence, even worse than the cries because it carried such a weight of expectant horror.

Then, the final scream.

Helen screamed with it. She was sobbing, tears running down her cheeks, and she could not help herself. She threw her head back and screamed, her scream outlasting and obliterating that other one.

From somewhere out there, beyond her door, a voice spoke her name. Her scream broke off in her throat, became a strangled, gasping cry. She looked and saw her door opening, and even while her heart went pounding, she thought, Now it comes, now I shall meet it face to face.

The door opened, light came in from the hall and, quite unexpectedly, Aunt Willa was standing there, feeling for a light switch where there was none.

'Helen,' she said again. 'Are you all right? What's wrong?'

'Aunt Willa,' Helen cried, and then she was

out of her bed, bounding across the room to fling herself into her aunt's arms, because she was glad to see even her, to see anyone real and human and warm. She sobbed against her aunt's silk-covered shoulder.

'Oh, God, it was awful,' she sobbed, clinging to her aunt. 'Do you know who it was? It was my mother. That was the way she died, laughing and screaming like that.'

'Helen, you're hysterical,' Aunt Willa said. 'Where the hell is the light switch?'

'There—the dresser,' Helen said, pointing. Surprisingly, she found herself laughing. She did not know why she should be, but she was.

Aunt Willa disentangled herself and went across the room. In a moment she had found the light, and its brightness sent the shadows scurrying.

Helen blinked and squinted, trying to get the room into focus. Its edges seemed too sharp, as they will after such darkness, the colors seeming to jangle oddly.

She sniffed and looked at her aunt.

'Now,' Aunt Willa said, 'what on earth happened? You scared me out of seven years' growth, screaming like that.'

Helen laughed nervously and wrapped her arms about herself. 'That wasn't me,' she said, almost giddy with relief that it was over. She had never imagined that she would be so ecstatically glad for Aunt Willa's company, but she was now. 'Only at the end. I did scream then. But all the rest of it, that laughing and screaming you heard, that wasn't me. That was mother. That was the way she screamed that night . . .'

She stopped abruptly and caught her breath. She did not know just what it was, but something in her Aunt Willa's face suddenly sobered her and made her stop babbling. She fell silent.

'What are you talking about?' Aunt Willa asked. 'What screaming and laughing?'

'Didn't you hear . . . ?' Helen stopped again. She had a terrible sinking sensation of falling down, down into an evil, waiting darkness.

She looked at her aunt, regarding her suspiciously, and it seemed to her as if there was more than the width of a room separating them; her aunt seemed to recede and withdraw, until there was a world, an entire universe between them, and when Aunt Willa spoke, her voice came from an eternity away.

She didn't hear. And this is just another nightmare. Oh, God, help me. Give me the strength to endure, or take this evil from me. I'm losing my mind. Help me. Someone help me, please.

'I heard you scream,' Aunt Willa said. 'That's what I heard. I thought . . . you must have been having a bad dream. Jesus, you scared me.'

CHAPTER ELEVEN

'Are you sure you want to stay here by yourself?' Aunt Willa asked. They had come into the hall. She had a suede car coat flung over her shoulders and was carrying the tote bag she had brought as an overnight bag.

'I'm not entirely by myself,' Helen said. 'Mrs. Halvorsen is here days.'

'I know, darling, but last night . . .'

'Last night I had a bad dream. Everyone has them from time to time. It would be silly to dwell on it.'

'Maybe,' Aunt Willa said, opening the door. 'But if you could have seen how awful you looked; and to tell you the truth, you don't look a whole lot better this morning. You're as white as a ghost . . .'

'I'm all right,' Helen said, unable to keep from sounding a little sharp. She was afraid that Aunt Willa might yet change her mind about going, and whatever else she had to endure, she was certain she could not endure that on top of it.

She had been, in fact, a little surprised, even puzzled, that Aunt Willa had gone ahead with her plans to leave this morning. She had a vague idea that Aunt Willa had scored some sort of triumph. Certainly her hysterical behavior during the night had given Aunt

Willa ammunition she could use if she chose to initiate any sort of legal manipulations later, and Helen wondered that her aunt had not chosen to follow this up.

After some consideration, however, she had hit upon the obvious truth. Aunt Willa was frightened. Not only her sleep but her usual poise had been shattered by the night's disturbance, and for the moment she was only too glad to be leaving this house.

Helen went with her down to her car. 'I don't see why Robie can't come and stay with you,' Aunt Willa said, getting into the car. It was a Mercedes, and had been part of her last marriage settlement. 'Did you ask her?'

'No,' Helen said. 'I wanted to be by myself. I wanted everyone to see that I was perfectly all right now, that I didn't need to be taken care of like an infant.'

It was a pointed remark and Aunt Willa, starting the motor and putting down the window, did not fail to get the point. She looked out the window at her niece, letting her glance flicker up and down slightly as if she were sizing her up.

'But *are* you all right, really, dear?' she asked. 'I mean, maybe you do need someone to look after you. You did scare the devil out of me, you know, screaming like a banshee. It seems to me that if you can't get someone to stay here with you, maybe you should go somewhere. You know, somewhere where you'll have people to look after you.'

'I don't need people to look after me,' Helen said firmly, because now that her aunt was actually in the car, with the motor going and obviously getting ready to leave, she had a bit more courage about facing up to her. 'I want to take care of myself. And there's nothing crazy about that.'

Aunt Willa lifted one eyebrow slightly. 'Well, no one said you were crazy, I'm sure. I certainly never used that word.'

Helen stepped back from the car. 'Goodbye, Aunt Willa, it was kind of you to have come,' she said.

Aunt Willa hesitated for a second or two, about to say something more, and then thought better of it. 'Goodbye,' she said. 'I'll stop back again in a little while and see how you're doing.'

'You should call before you come,' Helen said. 'I may be away or something.'

Aunt Willa's head snapped around. 'Are you planning to go somewhere?' she asked.

Helen, who had only made the remark to discourage another unexpected visit, felt amused and she said mischievously, giving a shrug, 'I don't know. I may do some traveling. I have all that money now, I suppose I may as well use it.'

Robie had told her that Aunt Willa had been decrying a shortage of money lately that had stood in the way of a trip she had wanted to take to the Riviera.

Aunt Willa's lips tightened a little, but she managed to say in a civil voice, 'You may as well,' and without further comment she drove off down the driveway.

Inside, Mrs. Halvorsen was dusting. Helen had the impression the housekeeper was watching her out of the corner of her eye. No doubt she had heard of the night's 'bad dream.' Perhaps she had been recruited to keep an eye on her and report to Aunt Willa.

Helen went through the house and out onto the terrace. Her nerves were stretched taut. Before her the hours of the day were a torturous path that led to another night, and God alone knew what fresh terrors. She did not know what she should do. Several times she made up her mind that she must do as everyone advised and leave the house. But she was unaccustomed to taking action, and as quickly as she reached this peak of decision, she slid back into the valley of indecision.

She put off doing anything. Twice she went back into the house, meaning to telephone Robie and ask her to come down so she could discuss all these matters with her. The second time she got all of the digits to Robie's phone number dialed except for the last one before she replaced the telephone receiver in its cradle.

Robie would think she was crazy. No amount of sisterly affection or responsibility would prevent her from reaching that conclusion. Robie was the only person in the world who could be said to be on her side. She could not bring herself to risk that loyalty; not just yet.

She went back to the terrace and sat watching a solitary blackbird hop and step about the edge of the terrace, turning his head this way and that as if he were looking for something he had lost. She thought his expression looked unhappy and it occurred to her that he was alone, with no companions in sight.

'We're alike, you and I,' she said to him. 'Lonely and unhappy. What on earth are we going to do about it?'

For an answer he suddenly leaped skyward. The sound of her voice had perhaps startled him, and he disappeared overhead. She felt strangely saddened to see him go. She thought it was a very unkind deity who would have put them both into this unhappiness and given only one of them the power to fly away from it.

'Did you say something, Miss?' It was Mrs. Halvorsen, at the French doors.

Spying on me, Helen thought. 'No,' she said aloud. 'I was just talking to a bird.'

'A bird, Miss?'

'It flew away,' Helen said, thinking that that ought to be obvious.

In the end, she decided to do nothing until she had seen what happened this night. What if Aunt Willa had been right, and it had only been a dream? However real it had seemed to her, it might have been a dream, might it not? Some dreams did seem that real.

She would wait one more night and of one thing she was certain: Tonight she would not dream. If anything should happen, she would know.

Then, if she must, she would call Robie.

* * *

Nothing happened. Nothing.

She took one of the tranquilizers that Doctor Ida had given her before she left the clinic, and deliberated over a sleeping pill before deciding against it. She wanted to stay awake. It was the only way she could really know. If it had somehow been just a dream, it could not trouble her if she were awake; and if it were not a dream, then she was better off being awake to cope with it.

She sat and read in the chair in her room, turning it so that it directly faced the door. She had locked the door with the big old key she had found in the kitchen, where the keys were always kept. She had considered placing her dresser against the door as well. She did not know if whatever she had heard in the house could get through locked doors; if it could, then it could no doubt get through dressers as well.

At first she read for a moment or two at a time, only to find herself watching the door expectantly, anxiously. But as the hours crept by and nothing happened, she became less concerned with the door.

Sometime late in the night she fell asleep. It was morning when she woke, and nothing had happened; she felt nearly giddy with relief.

Nothing happened the next night either, or the night after, or the night after that. It became apparent that however real the disturbances had seemed to her, they had indeed been only part of her dreams.

Her life did not suddenly become one of unbridled happiness as a result of this conclusion. Some of the tension disappeared, it was true, and she slept better, with no recurrence of the dreams.

But she still lived in her isolation, conscious of her separation from others. She still sometimes dreamed the old dreams, of being like other people, having friends, perhaps experiencing romance; but she dreamed them without hope that they would come true.

Sometimes she went out, a time or two to the cemetery, and again to shop in the local stores. She did this more than anything else to try to accomplish some touch of oneness with the outside world, with other people. She had talked briefly to Robie of her old wish to be free, but she was no more free now than she had ever been. The past, her old habits, fear, the very makeup of her personality, imprisoned her and cut her off from the world as surely as if she had been invisible. Indeed, she began to think of herself that way.

Robie called several times during the next month. It was plain that Robie did not like telephones. She gave the impression of regretting what she regarded as her duty. Each time she called, she suggested that she could come for a visit if Helen needed her.

'It's not like I'm at the end of my rope,' Helen said. Robie's discomfort on the phone made her uncomfortable, too.

'Well, I can be there in practically no time if you need me. All you have to do is say the word.'

'Things are all right now. They were a little strange at first, but it's better now.'

'In what way, strange?' Robie sounded worried.

'Oh, look, don't you start psychoanalyzing me. I promise when we do get together I'll tell you all about it. Just now you'd think I'm crazy.'

Robie laughed and said, 'I guess as long as you can make remarks like that, you aren't. But you will call if—well, if anything. Promise?'

Aunt Willa did not call. Helen supposed Mrs. Halvorsen kept her up to date. Truth to tell, Mrs. Halvorsen's reports must be very disappointing, unless she embellished them a bit, which seemed unlike Mrs. Halvorsen.

Nothing happened.

Miss Clark—the older of the two Misses Clark—came once for a call. She had not been in the habit of calling in the old days, and for a good reason. Helen's father had called her an unqualified snoop, and forbidden her to come. But Miss Clark had no reason to suspect Helen would know about that.

Helen dutifully invited her in and gave her tea, and pretended not to notice the piercing looks Miss Clark shot around the vestibule as she entered. It was almost as if she thought the bodies might still be lying there awaiting her inspection.

'You don't mind being here by yourself?' Miss Clark wanted to know while she sipped her tea.

'Why should I mind? Won't you have one of these cookies? Mrs. Halvorsen made them herself.'

'She's so wonderful, isn't she, so loyal. Standing by you through everything, and you know she must be scared to death to come back up here to work. I heard you weren't well. I heard you had to have a long rest.'

'It was a bit of a strain,' Helen said.

'But you're all right now?' Miss Clark said it as if she did not believe it.

'I am all right, thank you. More tea?'

Except for Miss Clark's visit, nothing happened. Not for a full month.

* * *

This time it was her father. She sat shivering in her bed and listened to the ruckus outside her door. She heard all the yelling and the shouting and the crashing of furniture and even the gunshots. Because she had been through it all before, she could follow in great detail the progress of the struggle, from its inception right through to its grim conclusion at the foot of the stairs.

She was sick with fright. But at least they did not come into her room. She was spared that reenactment. She could even tell in fact when it was over, because the awful cold that had come into her room and awakened her lessened, and the room grew warm again.

She had learned one thing, though. It happened with the full moon, just as on that first night, the night it had actually happened, when there had been a full moon.

So she had a month in which to get help.

PART TWO

ROBIE

CHAPTER TWELVE

'So why does she have to come here? If she's got all that goddamned money, why can't she go stay at a hotel someplace?'

He was a big man, bulging with muscles and a beer belly that distorted the line of his tee-shirt. Despite several years of college, which he had spent playing football, he was not very intelligent.

'It wasn't his mind that appealed to me,' Robie was fond of explaining to her friends. 'He has all the right instincts.'

'Because,' she said now, addressing him as one would a stubborn child, 'she is my sister, and she is coming to visit me for the first time ever. Look, Joe, it won't hurt you in the slightest. And I'm paying for your room, right?'

'Wrong. This is my room,' he said with an emphatic sweep of one beefy hand. 'Why can't I stay here anyway? What the hell, doesn't she know about boys and girls?'

She smiled a little wryly. 'Frankly, I don't think so. Take my word for it, we would all be uncomfortable. Now be reasonable. And hurry, she'll be here in a minute.'

'It's damn short notice,' he grumbled, shoving some jeans into a canvas flight bag that was all his luggage.

'It's short notice for me, too,' she said. She had not even known Helen was coming until she was virtually here, calling from the station to say she had decided upon a visit. And something about Helen's voice, about the nonchalance and the unnatural brightness of it, had told her that Helen needed her in some way. So, like it or not, Joe had to go. If something was bothering Helen, Joe's presence would certainly inhibit her from talking about it.

Still grumbling, Joe allowed himself to be shepherded out the door, on his way to a small rented room a block away.

'When will I see you?' he asked, pausing in the doorway.

'When I can,' she snapped, and then, seeing the hurt expression in his quite childlike eyes, she stretched on tiptoe to kiss him. 'Silly, do you think I won't miss you, too? I'll get together with you, somehow.'

Helen arrived minutes later, looking flushed with the excitement of making her own way there in a taxi from the station. Robie saw that she was very keyed up, more than from just the trip. But she let it go for a while, and kept up a flow of welcoming chatter while Helen settled in, taking off her coat and hat and gloves, freshening up in the tiny bathroom.

'. . . Such a wonderful surprise,' Robie said from the other room. 'I'd have been happy to have you up sooner, but you sounded so determined about staying in that gloomy old house. What changed your mind anyway?'

Helen went back into the combination living room-bedroom. 'Nothing in particular. I just thought maybe a few days in the city would—I don't know. Would something.'

'And they will, too,' Robie said, putting an arm about her. 'Do you know this is the first lime you've ever come to visit me in all these years.'

'I couldn't before,' Helen said.

'I know, he'd never have permitted it. Are you hungry? How about some lunch?'

'Fine.' Helen paused and then said, 'Robie, about your friend . . . I could stay at a hotel, you know. I didn't mean to put him out. To tell the truth, I forgot about him.'

'My who?' Robie looked blank for a moment, then laughed and gave a gesture of dismissal. 'Honey, you're so cute when you try to skirt issues. He's not my friend, he's my lover. Anyway, he moved out ages ago. He didn't just leave so there would be room for you. Now don't you worry about him. What in heaven's name made you think of him, anyway?'

'When he moved out ages ago, he forgot to take his shaving things out of the bathroom cabinet,' Helen said with a smile. 'The razor's still warm.'

Robie looked surprised. She went into the bathroom and saw for herself that Joe had left behind his electric razor, his colognes—everything of his that had been there. Probably left it on purpose, she thought. When she came back out, she had a mock guilty look.

'Well, maybe he's growing a beard,' she said with a shrug. She laughed and hugged Helen and said, 'Let's go out and eat something. You'll suffer through my cooking soon enough. And believe me, it will make you look upon Halvorsen in a new light of affection.'

'I don't think anything will accomplish that,' Helen said, wrinkling her nose.

They had lunch in a shiny little eating place that advertised 'Hidden Health'; none of Helen's dishes, ordered for her by Robie, were quite recognizable, but at Robie's prodding, she shook her head and agreed they were very good. The restaurant was owned by a friend of Roble's, a male friend. All of Robie's friends, it began to appear, were male.

Watching her sister, Helen envied Robie her easy confidence and the natural flow of conversation, even with strangers. Robie was as casual and breezy with someone who had just come in off the street as she had always been with Helen herself.

Helen could not talk freely, not even with Robie. She had come up to the city on an impulse, telephoning Robie with the excuse that she had an urge to see New York. The truth was that she had no one else in the world, other than Robie, to whom she could turn, and she knew that she must do something.

The house—her house, in which she had been raised, and which was now her home—was haunted. Or, alternatively, she was out of her mind. But she did not like to consider that alternative. She was convinced that she had seen what she had seen, and heard what she had heard. Something was manifesting itself in that house, something that was supernatural.

She had never asked herself before whether she believed in the supernatural, in ghosts and the like. Never before had there been any need to consider the matter.

Now there was clearly a need. She could not but believe. She had heard the voices of her parents: her mother laughing and sobbing hysterically as she died whatever gruesome death she had died; her father, shouting and swearing as he was killed fighting off his attackers. She had heard these voices, replaying as it were their parts in that grim drama long after the actual events had occurred.

Her parents were in their graves, but something, something of them, lingered in the house, haunting her. This was real, or she could no longer trust her mind at all.

How could she tell Robie these things, though? She sipped something that Robie described vaguely as a 'protein drink,' and looked across the little metal table at Robie.

Robie, with her bright eyes and her dyed hair, and that too-crimson lipstick smeared across her mouth in a haphazard slash. Robie was alive, utterly alive; what traffic did she have with the dead?

Robie, who had watched these various thoughts chase one another across Helen's face, suddenly put her cup down with a bang and said, 'You're going to have to tell me sometime.'

Helen started and said, 'What?'

'Something is bugging you. You've been sitting there for fifteen minutes not listening to a thing I've said, and stewing over something. Now tell big sister what it is.'

'I might just have come to see you and the city,' Helen said, putting it off. She looked down at the muddy liquid in her cup. It looked as bad as it tasted.

'Oh, sure,' Robie said drily. When Helen did not reply at once she said tentatively, 'It's Aunt Willa, isn't it?'

Helen's eyes went wide. 'Aunt Willa?' she repeated.

'She came to see you. And she bugged you,' Robie said. She had the air of a woman who was satisfied she had learned what she wanted to know. She had put this explanation together in her mind the last few minutes, watching Helen. She was the sort to let Aunt Willa get under her skin.

'Look, honey, she called me. I know all

about everything you did while she was there, including the fact that you had a bad dream. For Christ's sake, Joe usually has to punch me once a week to wake me up from some creepy crawly I'm dreaming up. It's nothing to get into a blue funk over.'

Tell her, tell her, a voice shrilled inside Helen's head.

'Am I right?' Robie persisted confidently.

'I guess you're right,' Helen said.

'All you need is a chance to relax a little,' Robie said, pleased with herself. 'I'm so happy you've come up to town. We're going to have a ball, the two of us, and you won't ever want to go back to that gloomy barn. And if you have a bad dream while you're sleeping with me, I shall simply kick you in the butt and tell you to be quiet.'

Partly because of the tension she had been under, and partly because she knew Robie would do just what she said, Helen began incongruously to giggle. The giggle became rapidly an honest-to-goodness laughing fit, in which Robie was only too happy to join. This was what she had wanted, to get Helen laughing, to make her forget Aunt Willa, and that gloomy house, and bad dreams.

The two of them sat leaning across the table, laughing, Helen trying to smother her laughter behind a lace handkerchief because she could see people were looking at them. Robie didn't care at all if anybody looked.

Helen's face was streaked with tears by the time she finally got herself under control again. But when Robie said, her voice sliding off into another howl, 'And I shall wear my hiking boots to bed,' they were off again.

This is ridiculous, Helen told herself, and very unladylike. But she laughed on, until she had exhausted the last of her meager store of laughter.

Across from her, watching despite her laughter, Robie thought, Isn't this wonderful? This is all she needed.

When they were more or less themselves again, Robie said, 'Come on, let's do some sightseeing. When were you last in town?'

'We came in with father the last time about ten years ago,' Helen said, collecting her purse and her gloves from the table.

'And with him, I'm sure you didn't get to have any fun. We'll make up for that, though, I promise you. It's going to be nothing but fun, your whole visit. I forbid a single serious thought.'

And so, Helen told herself, I cannot tell her about it, not now anyway. Not after that command, and when she's trying so hard to cheer me up. I'll tell her later, when it won't seem so serious. One night when we're in bed and we can laugh about it, and she will tell me how silly I am to be frightened.

It wasn't something she wanted to talk about, after all. She was glad of an excuse to put it off. And until she got ready to return home, it wasn't really important. That was when she needed to worry about it, and by then they would be at ease with one another.

She thought fleetingly, Robie is already at ease. But I may never be.

She did not let the thought linger. She waited by the glass door that led out of the restaurant while Robie went to the register to pay the check.

A fat woman came through the glass door, leading three children. The woman pushed Helen rudely out of her way, and one little boy stepped on Helen's foot without saying excuse me.

When Robie came up to her, grinning, Helen said, 'That child stepped on my foot.'

'They get busy here. The food is so good, and it's good for you. That's the wonderful part.' Robie was used to New York and boys who stepped on feet, and it did not even occur to her that Helen attached any significance to the incident. It was such an unimportant thing.

'He didn't even apologize. Think what father would have had to say to that,' Helen said.

Someone came between them as they went outside, and Helen had to take a little running step to get alongside Robie again. Robie walked very fast. It was the way she was used to walking, and everyone she was used to walking with kept up with her.

'Do you have any idea what they do to vitamins and minerals at Horn and Hardart?'

Helen didn't know who or what Horn and Hardart were, but it was impossible to ask, because now they were in a crush of people on the sidewalk, and it took all of her effort just to stay with Robie and not be swept away from her in the tide.

Once a young man going by with some friends took hold of her arm and tried to pull her along the other way. She was startled and frightened, but she had never in her life pulled away from anyone, and so she went, walking clumsily backward and feeling not only frightened but, far worse, foolish.

'Please,' she said, and stopped when someone bumped into her, knocking the breath out of her.

'It's all right,' her captor said. He was good looking in a slick, indolent way, with dark wavy hair and vivid eyes, and lips that looked almost as if he had lipstick on. She thought he was probably twenty. He looked actually younger, but there was something old about his eyes.

One of his friends said something she couldn't hear over the wailing siren of a passing police car, but the group of men all laughed, and looked hard at her. Another came around to her other side, taking that arm, and she was actually being carried away by them.

'We're the five musketeers,' the leader, the

one who had grabbed her first, said. 'We specialize in rescuing frightened young ladies in distress. You are a frightened young lady in distress, aren't you?'

He laughed and the one on her other side laughed, too, and said, 'She's a doll, that's what she is. We have found ourselves a doll.'

She didn't even try to answer his question, but yes, certainly she was frightened. All those faces going past, some of them laughing or angry or grimacing, flowing past like water, and she was anchored by the firm hands holding her.

'That's the really hard part about living in a city,' Robie was saying. 'That's the only thing I envy you, though, because . . .' And at that point she looked to her side, expecting to see Helen, and there was a stranger walking beside her on the crowded sidewalk.

She stopped short, almost knocking down a man behind her as she turned around. She saw Helen almost a block behind, being dragged along by a group of young hoods.

In a moment, Robie was beside them, looking like an avenging angel, and demanding in her most ringing voice, 'What in the hell do you think you're doing? Let go of her.'

No one, not even their father, had been unresponsive to Robie when she used that tone of voice. As easily as that, Helen's arms were released and she was free.

The one who had first seized her made a

low bow, despite the passing crowd, and said, 'Only trying to be of service. The lady looked lost and lonely.'

'Yes, especially lonely,' one of the others said, and they all laughed uproariously.

'I know what kind of service you had in mind, creeps,' Robie said. 'Bug off.' She felt in her purse for the small spray can she kept there and brought it out; she made a move toward the closest of the men, raising the spray can, but he put up his hands and backed away. 'Okay, okay, we're on our way,' he said.

They left, disappearing into the crowd, still laughing and occasionally looking back.

'Punks,' Robie said, and put the can back into her purse.

'What on earth do you suppose they meant to do?' Helen said.

'Helen.' Robie gave her a shocked look. 'I hope you aren't serious. Why in God's name didn't you fight them? They must have thought they had a very willing victim.'

'I didn't know what to do,' Helen said.

Robie sighed and shook her head. 'We're going to have a lot to do in the next few days, Come on.' She added emphatically, 'And stay with me, for Pete's sake.'

CHAPTER THIRTEEN

And they did do a lot in the next few days. Robie's chief medicine for any problem was keeping busy, and she set herself to keeping Helen busy seeing the city.

It seemed to Helen as if they must have seen everything that was even remotely worthwhile in the city, plus a few things that were not. Everything was seen in short, rapid little bursts of exploration, because that was the way Robie did things.

'We won't want to linger,' she would say, leading a brisk path through the Fulton Fish Market. 'We just want to get the flavor, so to speak.'

'But why should I want to see a fish market? I don't even eat fish,' Helen objected; her question went unanswered.

Helen was certain they had ridden every subway in the city. They pushed and raced through Times Square—'We won't spend any time here; it's gotten just awful anyway'—and were shot, as if from a cannon, in a high-speed elevator to the top of the Empire State Building. Robie, who had been here before and was getting a little tired of sightseeing, took a quick peek over the railing before whisking them down again in the fast elevator.

They saw Radio City Music Hall, but not for

the movie, just long enough to catch part of the show.

Only the ride on the ferry to the Statue of Liberty moved at a reasonable pace, and Helen thought from the way Robie kept peering down at the dark-looking water that she would have preferred to get out and swim to get there faster.

'There's so much to see and do in this city,' Robie said, trying to revitalize enthusiasm. 'Isn't it exciting?'

'It's certainly . . .' Helen paused, not sure just what she thought the city was. '. . . busy,' she concluded lamely.

It was entirely different from what she remembered from visits with her father. Of course those visits had been conducted at a very leisurely pace; not even the pace of life in Manhattan could have daunted her father, or altered his life style. And she, Helen, had seen everything from within a solidly insulated glass cage, seeing out, seeing everything, or as much as father gave her permission to see, but not touching anything, and never, *never* being touched—like when people ran into her now, on the sidewalk. She had stopped complaining to Robie about it, because Robie only said, 'It's a big city,' or 'Everything is so full here, even the sidewalks.'

The city was to Helen a jumbled impression, blasting loud and brilliantly lighted, and all rushing swiftly past and about her, always going in exactly the opposite direction from the one in which she was traveling. It did seem to her that no one, nothing was ever traveling in the same direction as she, although of course that was only her imagination. And if she tried to stop, tried to stand still for a moment to get her bearings, all that motion and activity whirled and eddied about her, like water in a river rapids surging about a rock, until it had dislodged it and could move it along as well.

'I never thought to ask,' Robie said, turning to look at her expectantly. 'Is there anything in particular you want to do?'

'Sit down somewhere and prop my feet up,' Helen said a little ruefully.

Robie laughed and said, 'You are so funny. I think it's done you a world of good being here.' She had been thinking all day how much better Helen looked. Of course, she herself had problems; Joe, for one.

They were in a taxi, rushing through Central Park on their way to a cocktail party. It was Sunday afternoon and Helen felt as if she had not had a chance to rest since she had arrived.

'We're not to mind the neighborhood,' Robie said, leaning toward the window to peer out at the houses going by. 'Lisa has been looking for months, and she was lucky to get this. Apartments are scarce, unless you've got a fortune to spend. You wouldn't believe how long I looked for that dump I'm in.'

Helen knew it was only her imagination in thinking that that phrase, 'Fortune to spend,' was emphasized. Robie would never emphasize that; she knew, after all, that she could have anything she wanted. Helen had told her that, right from the beginning.

'Robie, you know if you ever need anything,' she began, but Robie interrupted her, tapping on the glass that separated them from the driver.

'This is it,' she told the driver, as if he needed instruction, although in fact he was already slowing down for the address.

They went up three flights of stairs, narrow and dark. 'Never mind how it looks out here,' Robie said, panting a little. 'It'll be cute inside. Lisa is very clever, really; you know the type, does everything herself.'

Inside, the walls were lined with bookcases made of bricks and unpainted boards of plywood, and the furniture was studio beds piled high with assorted pillows and coffee tables that were really old trunks, or a wooden packing crate that had been used to ship liquor. When she put her drink down upon the latter, Helen got a splinter under her nail, and was embarrassed to tell anyone for fear of sounding as if she were criticizing Lisa's decorating.

'It's charming,' Helen said, when Robie prompted her with, 'Don't you love Lisa's apartment?'

There were other people there, too, and more arriving at frequent intervals. They drank a lot and talked extravagantly. Helen listened quietly, making only brief comments such as 'Nice,' or 'How true,' when prompted by Robie.

Even if she had been more of a conversationalist, and she was the first to admit she was not, Helen could not have contributed much. The conversation was mostly about New York, but a different New York from the one she had seen so far. It was about a showing at some gallery that she thought at first she would have liked to have seen, but decided otherwise when the others began to describe the sculpture.

They talked, too, about the theater, especially about the people in the theater. There were many names Helen recognized, but these people talked as if they were on intimate terms with the famous; especially they seemed to know all their weaknesses and foibles. They talked of the opera, and they talked of a party from the previous weekend.

The room got very noisy and very full. The air was close, and the conversations had become all muddled and fragmented, so that Helen, trying to follow them all, could hardly keep clear in her mind who was speaking to whom.

Robie drifted away from her. A young man elbowed his way through the throng to Robie's side.

'You're sure popular,' he said. 'This is the first I've been able to get close to you.'

She smiled up at him, an idea coming into her mind. 'Hi, Larry, you're just the person I wanted to see.'

He brightened and said, 'I am?'

'Yes. I want you to talk to someone . . .' He groaned. 'No, now really. It's my sister, and she's adorable, really; you two will hit it off just great.'

'I thought you and I hit it off just great,' Larry protested.

She lowered her lashes slightly and looked up at him through them. 'We do, silly, but this is a favor for me. Will you do it?'

His resistance melted in the warmth of her gaze. 'What exactly do you want me to do? Which one is she, anyway?' He strained to see where she had been sitting.

'In the gray dress. Just talk to her for a while, that's all.'

'If I do, will I see you later?'

She nodded and smiled coquettishly.

'What'll we do?' he asked.

'Well, I suppose you'll be tired of talking. We'll have to think of something different.'

In a moment she appeared before Helen, with Larry on her arm.

'Helen, this is Larry. Larry, my little sister. Larry has been standing over there ogling you for hours, so I told him he might as well come over and ogle at close range.'

'Robie, really,' Helen said, embarrassed.

'Well, it's true,' Robie said. 'Now, Larry, you sit right there next to her and see as much of her as you like. I promise she won't bite. I'll be back in a little while.'

Helen started to stand. 'Are you leaving?' she asked, alarmed at the thought of being left on her own in this sea of gesturing people.

Robie pushed her gently but firmly back down. 'Never you mind about me, you just relax and enjoy this young man's company. I have to talk to someone.'

Helen tried to watch to see where she was going, but the young man seated beside her distracted her, and when she looked again Robie was out of sight.

'You're a lot different from your sister,' he said, looking her up and down in a rather rude fashion.

She did not know whether that was intended as a compliment or not, and she hardly knew how to answer. 'Yes, I suppose I am,' she said, and tried to look for Robie again, but by now Robie had completely disappeared.

'Is this your first trip to New York?' Larry asked.

Helen turned her eyes on him. He did not look at all like he was ogling her, not even giving him the benefit of her inexperience in such things. He looked, in fact, rather put upon.

‘Not exactly,’ she said, taking a violent and inexplicable dislike to him. ‘Look, Mr . . .’

‘Larry,’ he said, smiling, but only with his mouth. ‘Call me Larry.’

‘Mr. Larry, I think I’ll get up and walk around a bit; I’ve been sitting in this one spot since I arrived.’

‘I’ll come with you,’ he said, without any warmth.

‘It isn’t necessary,’ she said. She had already stood, and she gestured for him to remain where he was.

‘Robie told me to keep an eye on you for a while.’

His eyes told her quite bluntly that this was no pleasure for him either. She felt her face burning, but she managed to keep her voice steady and said, very emphatically, ‘It isn’t necessary.’

She did not wait for him to argue further (he didn’t look as if he meant to anyway; no doubt he felt he had fulfilled his obligation to Robie) but drifted away in the crowd. It was like a thick fog, all those people, parting to let you move, drifting closed behind you, swallowing you up. In a moment she could look back and Larry had disappeared in the fog.

She had been introduced to countless people; so many, in fact, that she could remember no one. Here and there a face was familiar, but she could attach no names to them and so she did not try to attach herself to any of them either, but continued to drift in the direction of the window.

The window was shut, despite the thick smoke filling the room. She tugged at it, trying to get it open, but it wouldn't budge.

'It doesn't open,' a man said beside her.

She looked over her shoulder. He was thick and pink-faced, and he was ogling. 'You'd think,' she began lamely, but shrugged the rest of the sentence off. Her hands had gotten dirty from the windowframe. 'All this smoke . . .'

'Not a safe neighborhood,' he said, parts of his speech being drowned out by the din in the room. '. . . someone always getting robbed or killed . . . keep things locked up tight . . .'

'Is it that bad?' she asked. She was thinking, Why, isn't that funny, our neighborhood is entirely different from this, and they came in there to rob and kill; and locked windows did not keep them out, either. Ours was a safe neighborhood.

She put her face close to the glass and looked down. There was someone lying, apparently asleep, on a doorstep across the way. There was garbage in the street, and half a block down some children were playing, or fighting, she couldn't tell which.

Someone came into view below. A girl. She lifted her hand to wave at an approaching taxi, and in a moment the top of her bleached head had disappeared into the cab and she was gone.

'Robie,' Helen said aloud, incredulously, and then again, 'That was Robie.'

She literally pressed her nose against the glass, looking after the cab, but it was gone from sight in a moment.

She told herself that surely she was mistaken. Robie wouldn't have just gone and left her here to . . . to whatever might happen to her.

She looked around, straining up on her toes, as if at any moment she would see Robie emerging from the fog bank. She saw neither Robie nor anyone she knew.

'Pardon me,' she said to the lady nearest her, whom she was certain she had not met. 'I wonder, do you know Robie—Roberta Wren? She's my sister.'

'Is she in the theater?' the woman asked, eyeing her a bit strangely. Helen had gotten her nose smudged with black where she pressed it against the window.

'I don't think . . . no, she isn't, not in the theater,' Helen stammered.

'I don't know the name,' the lady said, and turned her back.

Helen decided she would go back to Larry; he could tell her, surely, if Robie had planned on leaving or what.

But she couldn't find Larry either. When she finally got to where she had left him, he was nowhere in sight. Nor could she find Lisa, her hostess, nor anyone who seemed to know Robie.

She had a strange feeling that maybe she did not belong here, that maybe she *wasn't* here. Maybe she had dreamed it all, the way she had dreamed other things—dreamed of coming in with Robie, meeting Lisa, being introduced to people. But if none of it was real, if she wasn't here, where was she?

Her head began to ache terribly and people looked at her so oddly when she tried to talk to them. The air was thick with cigarette smoke, and she had had more to drink than she had ever had before.

'Is there something wrong?' one man wanted to know when she asked if he could help her find Robie.

'No, only I thought I saw her leaving,' she said.

He looked at her oddly too. 'Well, if she left, then she isn't here,' he said, and drifted away. He was carrying two drinks, one in each hand.

Finally, she left, too. Even if the room and the party and all the people weren't real, Robie's apartment was, and if she were having a dream, then she had only to go back to reality, to any point in reality, and then it would be all right.

It was not so difficult as she had thought. She had watched Robie since she had been here and now, when she came out, she went directly to the curb and lifted a hand. As if it had been just sitting up the street waiting for her, a cab appeared, its door swinging open for her.

Robie had given her a key to the apartment, in case of emergency, she said, and it did not even occur to Helen to ring. She let herself in. The room was dark, and filled with a mysterious flurry of sounds. The light switch was on the wall near the door, and Helen reached for it.

* * *

There was all the darkness and the emptiness, and then Joe's voice and then Robie letting out the breath she had been holding in a long sigh.

'Oh, Joe, honey, I've missed you, too,' she murmured, clinging to him, absorbing the impatient rhythm of his body.

It was then that the light came on, and Roberta, twisting around to see past Joe's naked, muscular shoulder, saw Helen standing in the doorway.

Helen had never seen a naked man before. She stared. And he stared back, at first in surprise, and then angrily, while Robie, talking so fast and so shrilly it was impossible to understand her, scrambled for her clothes.

'Joe,' she said, gasping for breath. 'For God's sake, put on your pants.'

CHAPTER FOURTEEN

'I just don't understand why you didn't stay at the party. I thought you would stay there until I got back.'

Robie refilled her coffee cup and banged the pot back on the stove so hard that it rattled. She had, with considerable difficulty, managed to restrain her own temper and get a frustrated Joe quickly out of the apartment.

Helen put her hands to her burning cheeks and pressed, squeezing her mouth all out of shape. When they were little they had played that way, making faces, seeing who could be the most grotesque.

'I saw you leave,' Helen said. 'I was frightened in a strange place, with all those strange people. I don't suppose you have ever been frightened, but I have, and I can tell you, it is not pleasant. I didn't even try to think, I came straight here. I thought . . .' She paused, looking puzzled. 'I don't even know what I thought. I must have thought something.'

Robie looked at her sister; lips were pushed out in a distorted, puffy way. Her hair, which Robie had tried to restyle, fell across her forehead in limp strands that were not even as pretty as her usual casual hairstyle.

Robie sighed and some of the rigidity went out of her shoulders. She ought to have known how frightened Helen would be. She had never had a chance to get used to parties and people and a great deal of commotion.

'You could at least have rung the bell when you got here,' she said, more gently.

'I didn't think,' Helen said. She pushed the flesh up over her cheekbones, crushing her eyes into narrow slits of distorted flesh.

'I suppose now you'll be going home?'

'I'm afraid to go home,' Helen said matter of factly, opening and closing her eyes in a tentative way.

'Why should you be afraid of going home?' Robie asked. 'I mean, all that happened a long time ago. It can't happen again, you know.'

'It does, though,' Helen said.

'What does?'

'It happens again. And again and again and again. That whole, awful night happens again, every month.'

'What are you talking about?' Robie asked. 'Do you mean those nightmares of yours?'

'I mean the house is haunted.'

Robie's eyes widened and she set her cup absentmindedly aside. 'Do you mean you've seen ghosts?' she asked, watching her sister closely.

Helen took her hands away from her face and it fell into its familiar shape. She looked drawn and tired, and there were lines about her eyes caused by the fear that had been nagging at her constantly.

'Not seen,' she said, 'heard. I hear them: father, the others, all of them. I hear everything, just the way it happened that night.'

Robie slowly let his remark sink in. It was incredible to think that such a thing could happen, to Helen of all people. She, Robie, had no particular disbelief in ghosts; after all, she believed in other sorts of psychic phenomena, didn't she? She had a girl friend who was wonderful with horoscopes, and another who insisted she was a witch. And she herself had several times had experiences that she considered psychic.

But ghosts? And with Helen, who, one had to face it, had had some troubles recently.

She slowly pulled out a chair, never taking her eyes from Helen's upturned face, and sat at the table opposite Helen.

'Tell me everything about it,' she said.

As easily as that, Helen told her everything, from the first moments of her arrival back at the house, to the sounds she had heard, to the sense of brooding evil that she had felt with her almost constantly.

Robie listened attentively and quietly, interrupting just twice to ask questions. Her face revealed nothing but rapt attention. If she had displayed amusement, or disbelief, Helen would not have been able to continue. But because Robie seemed so unperturbed, she found herself talking more and more freely, actually feeling the burden being lifted from her shoulders as she related her experiences. It was so wonderful, just sharing it.

When she had finished, they sat in silence for a moment regarding one another across the small table. It was Helen who again broke the silence.

'Do you think I'm crazy?' she asked.

'Aunt Willa would certainly think so,' Robie said. She made a project out of finding and lighting a cigarette, blowing a cloud of blue-gray smoke into the air.

'What do you think?'

Robie said, thoughtfully, 'When I was at Columbia, there was a psychic who came to lecture one of my classes, a Doctor Buckley. Ghosts were sort of his specialty.'

Helen's face suddenly brightened. Her own thoughts had not gone that far. Faced with the fact of strange disturbances in the house, she had thought only of confirming them, by having someone else hear them, so as to prove that she was not insane. It had not crossed her mind that someone might want to investigate them, study them, learn what made them happen.

'Do you think he would be interested in this?' she asked aloud.

'Probably,' Robie said. She smoked rapidly for a moment. 'But first things first. I'm coming down to the house with you. I want to hear these happenings myself.'

'You think I'm imagining them?'

'Maybe,' Robie said frankly. 'The important thing is that this Doctor Buckley is very well known in his field, and if I'm going to go to him about this, I want to be sure of what I'm telling him. He might not be interested if he knew that the phenomena had only been heard by someone who . . . well, you know.'

'By someone who had had a nervous breakdown, you mean,' Helen said.

'We have to look at things honestly.'

'I understand. They are there, Robie. You'll hear them, too. And I'm willing to do anything that will persuade this doctor of yours to help us.'

Robie suddenly gave her an impetuous grin that made her look like a little girl. She ground out her cigarette in the ashtray.

'I think it's exciting, really,' she said. 'I've always wanted to see a ghost. It will be great fun, won't it?'

Helen managed a wan smile in response. She had been in the house during the manifestations. She did not think it would be great fun. But at least this time she would not be alone. She had been alone so much. Anything would be easier to face if there were someone there with her.

'We'll go down early,' Robie said, warming now to the subject with her customary enthusiasm. 'We'll make a party of it.'

Helen looked startled and said, 'Not with

other people?'

Robie laughed. 'No, just the two of us. I won't even let Joe come down to see me, so you won't have to worry about seeing him pantless again.'

She came impetuously around the table and hugged Helen. 'Oh, honey, it will be like we were little girls again, before anything went wrong.'

Helen thought, But it was always wrong; from the very beginning.

CHAPTER FIFTEEN

It took several days to return to the house. Robie went around her preparations as if she were planning an around-the-world cruise.

'Really, there's everything you need at the house already,' Helen pointed out.

'Maybe there's everything you need in that tomb,' Robie said, 'but I am used to a different life style.'

So it was necessary to go shopping, which Robie did with a vengeance. Helen tried to pay for her purchases, but Robie would not permit that either.

'That's where Doctor Buckley has his office,' Robie said one afternoon as they were leaving Hammacher Schlemmer, their arms full of packages.

'Who?' Helen asked.

'Doctor Buckley. The psychic investigator. He's a medical doctor, actually. Psychic phenomena is a hobby with him.'

'Maybe we should take him with us now,' Helen said. 'We could talk to him, at least.'

'When we get back,' Robie said. 'Taxi.'

There was a quarrel with Joe, who could not understand why it was suddenly so important that Robie accompany her sister home. Robie had promised Helen not to tell anyone the real reason, not until Robie herself had seen what was going on.

'If she doesn't want to stay here,' Joe argued, 'why can't she just go home alone? Why do you have to go?'

'Because she's been sick,' Robie said, 'and I don't think she should be alone just now.'

'Then hire her a babysitter, for Christ's sake.'

'Now, sweetie,' Robie said, and set herself to coaxing him out of his bad humor. She succeeded, but just barely, and only after promising she would stay no more than a month.

'That's all the time I could take off work anyway,' she said. That had involved another argument. Not that she particularly cared if they fired her; she was bored with the job anyway, and the boss was making noises that indicated he was interested in some after-hours activities, which did not interest her.

The last day before they were to leave Robie went out alone on a mysterious errand, the nature of which she would not disclose to Helen.

'You'll find out soon enough,' she said, and would explain no further.

She was back in a short while, holding something under her coat.

'Voilà,' she said, opening her coat to reveal a small brown and white puppy.

'A dog,' Helen said. 'But what on earth . . .'

'He's going with us,' Robie explained. She put the animal down, and he immediately began to explore his new surroundings, working his way cautiously closer to where Helen was standing. He was little more than a mutt, with large, friendly eyes and an active tail.

Helen was doubtful. 'I don't know,' she said hesitantly. 'You know how father always felt about pets in the house. And Halvorsen . . .'

'Father isn't there, not in the flesh anyway. And Halvorsen will fuss, but that's nothing unusual; she fusses all the time anyway.'

She did a comical imitation of Halvorsen's scowling expression and her irritated voice. 'I can't come full time, and I won't work at night,' she said.

Helen laughed and said, 'I suppose you're right.'

'I know I am. We need a dog. They're much more sensitive to spirits and things. If there's anything at all there, he'll sense it long before we do.'

'What's his name?' Helen asked.

Robie shrugged. 'Hasn't got one. I suppose we'll just call him Dog.'

* * *

At first it really was kind of fun. Robie's spirits were so buoyant, so infectious, that Helen found herself actually feeling gay and adventurous at being back in the house.

'We won't tell Halvorsen anything about the happenings,' Robie had dictated when they were driving down. 'She was scared enough about coming back up here. If she knew we even suspected there were ghosts in the house, she would set a new track record getting out of here.'

Robie made a joke of everything that had happened before, and because it was secret from Mrs. Halvorsen, or from anyone else for that matter, it became a source of great giggling and gesturing. Behind Mrs. Halvorsen's back, Robie would point silently at the bannister Mrs. Halvorsen was dusting, and then would wring her hands for Helen's amusement, as if wringing blood from them.

And Helen, who had been so terrified by just that occurrence, found herself laughing, laughing at herself, and she wondered now that she had ever been so frightened. The terror that the house had inspired in her now seemed unreal, and she began to wonder if perhaps she had imagined those events after all.

'We'll soon know,' Robie said when she confided these thoughts to her. 'Anyway, you have a good reason to be afraid, because if nothing happens on the night of the full moon, my pet, I am going to be ribbing you about this for the rest of your life.'

'In that case,' Helen said, 'I shall cover myself with a sheet and hover beside your bed during the night.'

'You'd better be careful to hover out of kicking range,' Robie said. 'I always go down fighting.'

The dog, still unnamed except as 'Dog,' met with Halvorsen's expected disapproval.

'I can't be responsible for what you find in your soup,' she said flatly.

'Within reasonable limits,' Robie corrected her.

Mrs. Halvorsen left the room in a huff, and the two girls giggled, Robie hugging the delighted animal.

The dog gave no evidence of sensing any foreign presence in the house. He quickly made himself at home, sharing the bedroom with the girls at night, and staying close to one or the other of them during the day. He seemed quite pleased with his new quarters.

It snowed as the month neared its end, the

first real snow of the season. Helen and Robie went out to play in the new-fallen snow, like a pair of children. They made a snowman and they threw snowballs at one another, and romped with the dog, and all three of them earned Mrs. Halvorsen's further disapproval by tracking snow into her clean kitchen.

The house, for all its poor lighting and antiquated design, actually seemed to absorb Robie's high spirits and for the first time it seemed a happy place, a charming old house that glowed and warmed. Fires burned in the fireplaces and in the evenings, after Halvorsen had gone, they would roast hot dogs and marshmallows, drink hot chocolate or munch popcorn, while the dog dozed on the hearth, and begged an occasional scrap of food.

And they talked. They talked of everything and nothing, and they avoided only one subject: their relationship with their father. As if by mutual consent, he never entered into theft conversation.

Later, Helen would remember that brief time of Robie's visit. It would stand out in her memory like an oasis in a desert, a brief breathing space. It was almost too beautiful. Despite the chill of winter and the snow that lingered on the ground, the days were sunny, the skies cloudless and a luminous silvery blue color.

Helen watched Robie play in the snow, chasing the dog, her yellow hair flying, her face flushed pink with the cold and with her laughter. For Helen it was wonderful just to sit and relax, to watch her, and think of nothing more than the passing moment. She felt wonderfully alive.

Robie had concluded that the 'ghosts' were nothing more than Helen's overworked imagination, and the strain she had been under. There had been nothing out of the ordinary happen since they had arrived. The dog was blissfully unaware of any hauntings. And Helen herself acted as if she had forgotten them.

'I shouldn't have left her alone down here, not at first,' Robie thought, and vowed she would be more considerate of her sister in the future.

All the while they played, the days passed by, liquid, hurrying, until it was nearly the end of the month.

As suddenly as if a switch had been thrown, it all changed. Helen woke one morning to find the world outside her window was gray and dreary. Tonight was the full moon, and the house, the sky, the whole world seemed to have just now remembered it, and been disheartened by the memory. The house, only the day before gay and cheerful, now seemed dark and gloomy, and from the shadows in the corners morbid fancies taunted her.

'Hey, come on,' Robie said when they were at breakfast. 'No long faces, okay? Nothing has changed since yesterday, you know.'

'But it has. Everything's changed. Can't you feel it, the tension in the air?'

'No, all I feel is your gray mood. That's the only thing that's changed. If you were like this before, it's no wonder you heard things.'

But everything had changed for Helen; even Robie had changed. She tried to perpetuate their mood of frivolity and adventure, but Robie's laugh rang hollow now, and as the day wore on, even she stopped pretending that things were the same.

'It's your fault, you know,' Robie said as evening darkened the rooms. 'You've been going around all day looking over your shoulder and jumping every time a board creaks. You've got me doing it. It's contagious. You've got to stop it.'

Robie was annoyed with herself for feeling jittery, and she blamed Helen. Helen was making her nervous; of course the place had the atmosphere of a haunted house. Helen herself was haunting it, with her fear.

'Don't you feel it?' Helen asked, instinctively lowering her voice as if someone might be listening, although Halvorsen had already gone for the day, and they were to all appearances alone with the dog in the house.

'There's a feeling of something there,' Helen insisted. 'As if you could turn and see it, almost; like someone whispering in the next room, whispers you can't quite hear, and yet you can, almost.'

'I don't hear or feel anything,' Robie said, a shrill note of anger creeping into her voice; this was really getting to be a drag. 'Except the tension you're creating by being so frightened. For God's sake, won't you relax and stop harping on what you imagine you feel?'

Helen could still feel it, though, and she was sure it was not just something she was imagining. There was something there, something as real as those screams she had heard, as real as the sounds of struggle outside her door. Something—she didn't know what to call it; a presence—that had not been there during the preceding days, but was there now. She could feel it in the rooms with them, she could almost hear what it thought. It knew that Robie was there; it knew that she was frightened, too, and did not want to admit it, because she had not yet seen or heard anything concrete. Robie was so practical.

But practicality, Helen thought, was not enough for some situations. Practicality would not spare them what was in store for them. She did not know what it was, but she was sure, as sure as she had ever been of anything, that the night before them would be like nothing they had ever experienced before.

CHAPTER SIXTEEN

She had been sure she would not sleep at all, but Helen did fall asleep with surprisingly little difficulty.

When she woke, it was gradually, and at first without knowing why. For a few seconds she lay in bed, listening to the silence, wondering what had awakened her.

Then, slowly, she became aware of the cold, intense, burning. She had wrapped the covers snugly about herself, and still she was shivering. Each second seemed to increase the cold.

She listened, and knew Robie was awake, too, and wondered what she was thinking now.

'Robie, oh God, you must be able to feel that,' she whispered into the darkness.

'I don't feel anything,' Robie's voice came back after a pause. But she sounded unconvincing. Her voice in the dark was tremulous and Helen knew that it was not only from the icy cold that had completely invaded the room.

'The cold. Oh, Robie, I'm freezing. I think I'm going to be sick.'

It was colder than it had ever been before, terribly, terribly cold, and she was more frightened than she had been before. She had a sudden knowledge that this was different, somehow, from all that had gone before.

Robie suddenly moved from her bed, came to Helen's bed, and hugged Helen in a protective embrace.

'It's all right, darling, really it is,' she said. 'Don't be frightened.'

'But don't you feel it, can't you feel the cold?' Helen clung to her, trying to absorb some warmth from Robie's body.

'Yes, I feel it, of course I do. The furnace has gone out, that's all. You're forgetting it's winter outside; in a minute I'll go downstairs and find out what's wrong with the furnace.'

She did not go, however, because in a moment the noises had begun.

Helen did not say anything, did not say I told you so. She held on tightly, as if she were sinking, and Robie was her last hope of salvation.

She knew every sound, every crash and bang, every cry of pain and horror, every woosh of knife cutting air. She tried not to listen, and wished something would stop the cold. She felt no warmth, even from Robie's arms around her. It was as if she were already dead, in the cold of the tomb, beyond the warmth of life. Icy curls of cold ran across her shoulders and along her spine.

Someone screamed aloud, 'For God's sake, please, stop it!'

With a shock, Helen realized it was she who had screamed aloud.

The noise did stop. The house suddenly sat about them in utter silence; not a board creaked, not a leaf beyond the window rustled.

'It's over,' Robie said in a cracking whisper.

Helen shook her head violently, and her body trembled convulsively with the cold that seemed to be growing worse. Never, not in her worst nightmares, had she dreamed it was possible to feel so terrified.

'It's not over,' she said. 'They are out there. They are listening. Robie, what are we going to do?'

'For one thing,' Robie said, taking a deep breath, 'we are going to turn on a light.' She started to get up from the bed, but Helen held on to her frantically.

'Don't leave me, oh my God, Robie, don't leave me,' she sobbed.

'All right, then, come with me, baby. I'm only going to the dresser.' Robie was trying to sound brave, but even her voice was quavery, and Helen could feel her shivering, too, beneath her nightgown.

They got out of bed together, a clumsy process because Helen would not relinquish her hold upon Robie's neck, and together they crossed the room to the dresser. The light switch clicked under Robie's fingers, and the light splashed into the room.

'Robie, look, the dog.'

Helen had forgotten that poor animal, but as the light came on, she saw him. He seemed to have been asleep, but now he sat up, his ears twitching, his nose sniffing. He fixed his eyes on Helen, and his stare was so strange that she found her attention riveted upon him. Slowly the dog rose to his feet, bristling, his stare even wilder, and he stood rigidly.

'The poor animal is terrified out of his senses,' Robie said, reaching out a hand toward him.

'Don't touch him,' Helen said. In the same moment, a cold wind blew through the room, as if a door or a window had suddenly been flung open, and they both whirled about, expecting to see the door standing open. It was still firmly closed.

It seemed like the door was far, far away, a mile or more from where they were standing. It seemed to Helen as if the very air between them and the door was churning.

We are lost, she thought. They are here with us, and it is over for me, I can no longer resist him. He can possess me, if that's what he wants; it's what he always wanted, what he always did, and I can no longer fight that.

'Don't say that,' Robie said. Helen did not realize that she had spoken aloud, or know what she had said, and she looked stupidly at her sister. 'Let me put you back to bed. I think it's over.'

'But you heard it, didn't you? You did hear it, Robie, say you did . . . oh!' She had looked back at the dog, and she saw that he had slunk into a corner of the wall as if to press his way through it. The animal was beside himself with fright, baring his teeth, his eyes huge in his tiny head.

Suddenly, the cold was gone. There was no rush of warm air; simply, it was no longer cold.

'Now it *is* over,' Robie said, and no sooner had the words come from her mouth than the laughing began. 'Lord,' she whispered. 'Who . . . ?'

She suddenly realized who, and jerked her head around to stare open-mouthed at Helen. 'No,' she said. 'No, it can't be.'

'Where are you going?' Helen cried. Robie had suddenly started across the room toward the door.

'It's mother, isn't it? It's coming from her room. I'm going to go see. I'm not going to spend the rest of the night cowering in here like a ninny. You can stay here, lock the door.'

'Don't leave me alone,' Helen begged, grabbing at her arm. 'I'd rather go with you than stay here alone.' Now that the cold was ended, she was not as frightened as she had been. Had they gone? She wasn't sure, but at least they weren't as vividly here as before.

When Robie opened the door to the hall, a fresh gust of cold air hit them, frightening Helen anew, but the hall was empty, and except for the laughing that they could hear more clearly now, the house was silent.

Wordlessly, Robie started along the hall

toward their mother's room. Helen took only a moment to observe that the door to their father's room was open. But not for anything would she have gone to that door and looked in. That was more than could be asked of human frailty. Looking from right to left, she followed closely along after Robie.

It was colder in the hall, colder as they approached the door at the end of the hall. The closer they came to their mother's room, the colder Helen felt again.

They reached the door without incident, and stopped outside it. The noise was still going on within. Someone—something—was laughing, actually roaring with laughter. There was no doubt that it came from within this bedroom. It was awful to hear it, to know that they were separated from the sound by a thin door.

Then, just as Helen had heard it before, only more distinctly because she was closer than she had ever dared be before, the laughter was cut, cut as if cut with a knife, and she heard a hiss of pain. She hadn't heard that before. It was too low to have carried as far as her room. And then they heard a gasp.

And finally, the shriek. It was a scream that came from the furthest depths of pain and torture. It was followed by groans and gasps. Helen thought she would faint. Her legs felt barely able to support her.

All this while, which may have been a

minute, perhaps two, she had watched Robie. Robie had said nothing since they had come into the hall, and so far she had not admitted to actually hearing anything. But Helen knew that she had heard everything, too. She had to hear it. And she was obviously frightened, despite her bravado. Her face was ashen and her eyes wide.

And then, silence.

'It's really stopped now,' Helen said breathlessly. 'It always ends after that.'

After a pause, Robie said, 'I'm going to go in there. I want to see.'

Helen grabbed her arm. 'No, Robie, no, please, for God's sake. It's over now. That's all there is.'

Robie turned to look at her. She even smiled, a bit shakily, and she looked less frightened than she had before. She was getting her courage back.

'It's all right,' she said. 'You stay out here. I just want to have a look. Is it unlocked?'

'I think so,' Helen said, nodding. 'I haven't tried it before.'

Robie put out a hand to the knob, and turned it. The door opened effortlessly, swinging in as if someone inside had opened it for her, inviting her in.

'Robie . . .' Helen started to say. Suddenly she felt colder than ever, freezing cold. She did not want to be left alone in the hall, and nothing could persuade her to go into that room.

'It's all right,' Robie said. 'You'll be all right out here. Wait here.' She went inside.

The door closed after her. Helen could not say if Robie had closed it herself, or some breeze—there was a draft here—had closed it. But a minute later, Robie said, from inside, 'Did you close the door?'

Helen said simply, 'No.'

She waited. The silence went on and on. From within she thought she heard footsteps, some hints of movement, but she could not distinguish them.

Abruptly and distinctly a voice, Robie's voice, but strangely changed, said, 'Helen, go away.'

Startled by the command, because it was given just as a command, Helen said, 'Robie . . .'

Robie did not let her finish, but interrupted her. 'I want you to go back to your bedroom, right now, and lock your door. Helen, do as I tell you.'

Helen hesitated for a moment, actually taking a step toward the door of her mother's bedroom, thinking, I ought to go in, I ought to see what's wrong.

From within, Robie said sharply, 'Helen, please.'

Helen went back along the hall toward her bedroom, looking over her shoulder at the closed door as she went. When she reached the open door of her own room, however, she stopped, and turned back to stare along the hall toward her mother's room. She could not think why Robie had ordered her away from that door; she was torn between her accustomed obedience to commands and her feeling that she ought to have gone in, to see what, if anything, Robie had discovered. She cursed herself for a coward and a fool.

At last, when she was on the verge of retracing her steps along the hall and inquiring if Robie was all right, the door opened. Robie came out, closing the door firmly behind her, and walked quickly along the hall. Helen stepped from her doorway, watching her sister approach.

She was struck by Robie's appearance. If ever she had seen horror in a human face, it was there. So altered was Robie's appearance that she might have met her on a crowded street, seen her, and not even recognized her own sister. She looked old and haggard, and in the dim light, utterly dissipated.

Robie was walking rapidly, almost running, straight along the hall. To Helen's surprise, she was looking straight ahead, and she did not stop as she neared Helen's bedroom, nor slow her pace in the slightest. She went without a pause toward the stairs, and only as she passed by Helen did she glance once, fleetingly, in Helen's direction, as if she had not before seen her.

In a whisper that seemed scarcely to come

from her lips, she said, 'For the sake of God, leave this place.'

A moment more and she was gone, rushing down the stairs toward the first floor.

Helen was so bewildered by this behavior she hardly knew what to do. She ran involuntarily to the head of the stairs, forgetting for a moment to be frightened, and called after her sister.

'Robie, wait.'

Robie did not wait, though. Clinging to the balusters and taking several steps at a time, she reached the floor below in a matter of seconds. Helen saw her fly across the vestibule, saw her fling open the door and rush out, not even bothering to close it in her wake. The heavy door swung to and fro in the icy wind that rushed through the house.

Helen was alone in the house.

And the house around her seemed to laugh silently.

CHAPTER SEVENTEEN

It was several long seconds before she could make herself move; then she began to run down the steps as Robie had done.

She had gotten halfway, however, before she stopped, remembering the dog in her bedroom. She could not go, no matter how frightened she was, and leave that poor terrified beast to an unknown fate.

She ran back up the stairs, trying not to think of what might be in the house with her. The dog was still cowering in the corner of her room. As she came in he again fixed his eyes on her with a look so wild that she hesitated to come all the way to where he was and pick them up.

'Come,' she said, but her voice was so tremulous that she knew it lacked any authority. The dog made no response; he might not even have heard.

She moved toward him, thinking she must try to pick him up and take him with her. She knew that he would never voluntarily come with her into the hall.

But before she could put a hand on him, a sound arrested her—the sound of a door opening.

Her first thought was that Robie had returned, that the night air had restored her to her usual calm good sense. Leaving the dog cowering in his corner, Helen started toward the hall. She heard footsteps beyond the door.

But at the door, still inside the room, she stopped again. The footsteps were not from the stairs, but from the other direction. They were coming from the direction of her mother's bedroom.

Whatever Robie had seen there, whatever had struck such terror into her, was coming along the hall toward her, Helen realized.

She stepped back and closed her door, turning the key in the lock. She was terrified. It felt as if the room had been turned to ice, and she clasped her arms about herself in a sudden frenzy of shivering.

How stupid she had been not to have realized; each time it had been more—more vivid, more complete. She should have realized that this time it would go beyond the others in some way.

She went back to the dog. That poor creature was in a dreadful state. He was pressed so tightly against the wall that she wondered if he had not hurt himself. She approached, wanting to gather him into her arms, not only to comfort him, but to take solace from the feel of living flesh next to her own, and so that they could face together whatever was to come.

But the poor animal was crazed with terror. He showed his teeth in a snarl, and would certainly have bitten her if she had tried to touch him. He did not even seem to recognize her.

In another moment she had forgotten the dog as a sound from outside stopped her, and she turned toward the locked door.

It was terribly cold, even colder than it had been before.

I am calm, she thought. Perhaps I am even dreaming this, as I dreamed those other things.

Or did I dream them? Is this what they mean by cold chills going up and down your spine? It starts all the way down, at my organs, and goes all the way up and back down, in flashes, like something alive.

She wanted to shout at it, to tell whatever was outside her door to go away. To ask, even, who or what was out there. But she had no voice with which to speak. Her voice was frozen inside her with the cold.

Robie, Robie, she thought, why did you leave me?

Nothing happened. The minutes dragged by. It might have been an hour, or only minutes, that she stood there, staring at the door, waiting for something to happen. She told herself that the intelligent thing, the right thing that Robie would do, would be to walk to the door, to turn the key in the lock and open the door, and face whatever was out in the hall.

Probably, she thought, there is nothing at all there, and an empty hall would relieve me of all this fear, and I could quietly pack up a few things and leave this house, and check into a hotel room somewhere in town for the rest of the night, for the rest of my life, even.

But she knew that, even if her feet would carry her across the room, nothing under God's blue heaven would ever make her open that door.

And finally, after she knew not how long of

waiting, there was a sound. Not, as she had expected, a knock or a rattle or a bang, but something far more terrible than any of those—a whimper.

Something outside whimpered, like a baby crying faintly, the way her mother used to cry when her father had done something hurtful.

It whimpered and scratched at the door; scratched on the wood with long fingernails.

She thought, I am going to scream. I cannot help myself, I am going to scream.

But she did not scream. She moved away from the door, stepping backward because she could not take her eyes from it, until like the dog she was pressed against the far wall.

She waited. And waited. And waited.

* * *

She did not know exactly when it ended. She was gradually aware of the room growing light with dawn; and suddenly she realized that the cold had gone. It was cool still, true, but that unearthly coldness had faded at some time or other without her quite being aware of it.

She began to rub the circulation back into her arms and to walk about the room. She looked at the door and listened, but she could hear nothing from beyond it, and finally she was sure that the ordeal was really over, at least for this one night. It took some minutes more, though, before she was able to summon the courage to cross the room and actually open the door to the hall.

There was nothing there. The house lay still about her, presumably empty. She had survived another onslaught of that terror, without, as it had developed, Robie's help.

And it would be the last such night, she promised herself. She meant to leave the house today, during the daylight hours, and she did not mean to return to it, ever. She did not care what anyone thought or said. And after all, what could anyone say or do? Robie had been here, too, and she had been frightened out of her wits, she could not deny that.

So she did not have to be afraid that the family would say she was crazy.

She felt a little lightheaded from lack of sleep and from the feeling of relief that the ordeal was momentarily over. She came back into her room and went to the window, flinging it open and breathing deeply of the crisp morning air.

She had forgotten about the dog, until her eyes fell on him as she brought her head back from the window. He lay in the corner where he had cowered during the night. She called to him but there was no movement.

With an eerie sinking feeling she went to where he lay. Before she had reached him, she knew that he was dead. His body was already cold to the touch. His eyes protruded; his tongue was hanging out of his mouth; the froth had gathered around his jaws.

The poor animal had died of fright.

*   *   *

She did not want to touch the dead animal, but she hadn't the heart to simply leave him lying there, frozen in his attitude of terror, until Mrs. Halvorsen came. She found a towel in the bathroom and, wrapping him in that, carried him to the kitchen with her.

By the time she had made herself coffee and warmed her still cold hands over the kitchen range, Mrs. Halvorsen had arrived.

'How do you suppose he died?' the housekeeper asked when Helen showed her the dog's corpse and asked her to have something done with it.

'He was like that when I found him this morning,' Helen said evasively.

'He looks scared, doesn't he?' Mrs. Halvorsen gazed for a moment at the wide, unseeing eyes. 'Oh well, I suppose it was something internal,' she concluded. 'I'll call the pound about him a little later. Will Miss Robie be coming down soon for breakfast?'

'Miss Robie has . . . gone out,' Helen said.

Mrs. Halvorsen gave her a surprised look. 'So early?'

'Something came up. Let's not wait for her, all right?'

'What time will she be back?' Mrs. Halvorsen asked.

What time? Where had she gone? Would she be back at all? Helen had questions enough of her own that she could not answer.

'I don't know,' she said simply. She thought to herself that there must be something she should do about Robie. She thought of calling the police, but the impossibility of explaining why Robie had bolted from the house prevented her from doing so. Robie had been beside herself. But surely she would come to no harm. She was an inherently sensible person, who had only been temporarily frightened out of self-control.

It was not necessary after all for her to call the police; they came to see her.

'There are some gentlemen here to see you,' Mrs. Halvorsen announced in awe. It was midmorning. Robie had still not come back or phoned, and Helen had grown increasingly anxious. She was pacing the floor in the den when the men arrived.

It was so unlike Mrs. Halvorsen to announce visitors formally, and it was so unusual for Helen to receive visitors, that she knew at once, instinctively, that something extraordinary had occurred.

She came into the hall to find two policemen waiting there. They wore highway patrol uniforms, and held their hats in their hands.

'Miss Wren?' The older of the two addressed her. He reminded her of her father; not so much the way he looked, as the way he stood, the way he spoke, the look he gave her—cool, commanding, stern.

'Yes,' she said, very softly, so softly that she felt compelled to repeat it a little louder. 'Yes?'

'Do you happen to know a Miss Roberta Wren?'

'Robie, she's my sister. Yes, what is it, has something happened?'

'There's been an accident,' the man went on, speaking in the same stern, uncaring voice as before. 'Your sister's car went off the road . . .'

She took a step toward him, reaching her hand out for him. She wanted to touch him, to assure herself of the reality of him, of this moment.

'Is she . . . ?' But she could not bring herself to ask the question that had come into her mind.

They mistook her outstretched hand and her faltering question. The younger of the two men moved toward her, clasping her firmly by the shoulders.

'Easy,' he said. He had a gentle-sounding voice and that, oddly, did more to restore her self-control than the other man's cold unemotionalism.

'I'm all right,' she said, taking a deep breath.

'Tell me what happened to Robie.'

'Your sister is dead,' the first officer told her flatly.

She had known actually from the moment Halvorsen had announced them, had known perhaps from the first moment that she returned to the house, that everything was moving toward something like this. She was more stunned than surprised.

'I see,' she said, and then because the patrolman still held her shoulders, she shrugged herself away from him and said, clearly, 'I am all right, really.'

The older patrolman said, 'I'd like to ask, Miss, if there was anything bothering your sister? A quarrel, maybe, or a fight with her boyfriend?'

She said, without the slightest hesitation, 'No, there were no quarrels. Why do you ask?'

'There was a witness to the accident, a man driving just behind your sister. He said it looked as if your sister had . . .' He faltered for just a moment. 'Had wrecked her car deliberately. Like she might have meant to kill herself.'

PART THREE

DOCTOR BUCKLEY

CHAPTER EIGHTEEN

It was not difficult to find Doctor Buckley's office. She knew from her conversation with Robie that he was a medical doctor and that psychic investigation was only a sideline. She knew that his office was in a building near Hammacher Schlemmer; Robie had pointed it out to her on a shopping expedition. She had only to read the directory in the lobby to find his office.

The receptionist, a brisk, mannish-looking woman, greeted her suspiciously.

'You don't have an appointment?' She repeated Helen's words in an accusing tone. 'The doctor is a very busy man. Perhaps if I made an appointment for you for, say, next Friday?'

'It's very important that I see him,' Helen said, and when the nurse's scowl deepened, she added quickly, 'It's not about a medical problem. It's a personal matter.'

That caused some deliberation, after which the nurse said, 'I'll see if he can spare you a minute. Come with me, please.'

She led Helen to a little cubicle of a room, an examining room, all white and stainless steel, and smelling vaguely antiseptic.

'Wait here,' she said, in a voice that implied she hoped it was a long wait. She went away, walking fast and with a military precision.

Helen waited; she had no clear-cut expectations regarding the man she had come to see. She had perhaps thought of him as pugnacious. Wouldn't one need to be to go into combat, even against ghostly things?

While she waited, she saw a small, pallid man going up and down the corridor, in and out of other examining rooms, and she supposed he was one of the doctor's assistants. She was very surprised then to discover that he was the man she had come to see. He was very mild looking, so soft-spoken that one could hardly hear him from across the room, and less ruggedly masculine than his nurse.

As for Doctor Buckley, he had no idea who this Miss Wren was who was waiting to see him. She had told his nurse she wanted to see the doctor on a personal matter, not a medical problem. But the name meant nothing to him. He had thought of several possibilities. A legal problem, perhaps a malpractice suit. But in that case, it would have been her lawyers who would have come to see him. The relative of a patient, concerned about the patient's condition; but again, the name was unfamiliar.

What he saw when he came into the room in which she waited was a rather pretty girl who, his expert glance told him, might need some medical attention after all; she showed all the signs of fatigue and hypertension. Probably, he deduced, she had been under some strain recently that had produced somatic effects.

'Miss Wren?' he greeted her. 'I'm Doctor Buckley. I believe you wanted to see me on a personal matter.'

He was carrying a clipboard with some loose papers on it, which he put aside reluctantly, a bit loathe to be distracted from them. He did not like having his professional time frittered away. He wondered if she would object to being charged for an office call.

She had only nodded when he greeted her, and he prompted her again, saying, 'What can I do for you?'

She cleared her throat and said, 'I'm Roberta Wren's sister.'

He frowned and she saw his eyes move ever so slightly toward the clipboard. She knew that he regarded her as an intrusion.

'I don't believe I recall . . .' he started to say.

'She was in a class at Columbia, and you came to lecture on psychic phenomena. I don't suppose you met her personally, but she was impressed by you, and did remember you, and she mentioned your name to me.'

'I see.'

If she had expected any surge of interest in hearing this clue to the nature of her visit, she was disappointed. He only continued to look at her in a questioning and not very interested way. He was mildly puzzled by her visit and her opening remarks, but nothing so far had greatly aroused his interest.

His lack of response, professionally intended to encourage his patients, had an opposite effect on her. She felt intimidated by it; for a moment she could not marshall her thoughts enough to say what she wanted to say. Again he prompted her.

'And your sister—Roberta, was it?—how is she?' he asked politely.

'Roberta is dead,' Helen said, and as if a dam had been broken, that statement of cold fact gave her the impetus to go on.

'They say she killed herself,' she said, talking rapidly. 'But that isn't true. She was driven to her death by, by something, I don't know what to call it. My house is haunted, horrible things are happening there. I thought it was because I was insane, but Robie heard them, too, and she saw them, saw something, I don't even know what, because I was too frightened to go in with her.'

This time she had indeed caught his interest. He listened to her rambling remarks at first with surprise, then with growing interest.

'Wait,' he said when she stopped for breath. 'There is something I must do. Please excuse me for a moment. Don't worry, I will be back.'

He went out, closing the door of the little examining room so that she would not be disturbed. He went directly to his nurse's desk.

'How many patients are waiting?' he asked.

She looked a little surprised, but she said,

'Mrs. Caldwell is in room number two. Mr. Adams is due any minute now. Then . . .'

'I'll see Mrs. Caldwell,' he said. 'After that, I don't want to be disturbed for an hour at least; tell the patients I have been called to an emergency, and if they don't want to wait, have them come back another time.'

She looked surprised, but she knew from experience not to argue. 'Yes, Doctor,' she murmured, casting a quick glance toward the room in which she had left Miss Wren.

It took perhaps ten minutes to dispense with Mrs. Caldwell in examining room number two. He knew that she would, if encouraged, ramble on for thirty minutes about her various aches and pains. He did not want to hear about them today. He wanted to be free to give this Miss Wren as much undivided attention as he could spare.

When he came back, she was pacing to and fro in the small area available to her. She looked frightened, as if she were afraid he did not believe her.

'Come with me, please,' he said, and led her along the corridor, past the other examining rooms, to his private office, a comfortable roomy refuge at the end of the hallway.

'I thought we would be more comfortable here,' he said. 'And I wanted to be sure we wouldn't be interrupted.'

He indicated a big worn-looking chair near his desk. 'Sit down, please,' he said, 'and do go on with your story. I find it most singular.'

Encouraged by his interest and his kindness, Helen found herself talking freely. There were no further interruptions. The doctor listened attentively as she told her story; she told it roughly, skipping about but touching upon the important points. It was such a relief to be able to talk about it, and his calm attitude was so reassuring that she talked more freely than she had ever talked to anyone before, even at the Villa de Valle, with all of its phony psychiatrists.

When she had finished telling him frankly about the last incident in the house, and Robie's fright, which had led to what might have been her suicide, she came to a pause and, looking across the desk at him, said simply, 'So you see, I do need your help.'

'Yes,' he said, almost absentmindedly. His thoughts in fact were elsewhere, on a story he had once heard, years before; it had been similar.

He asked, 'Exactly what do you think I can do for you, Miss Wren?'

'Why, I . . .' She stopped and thought. She had really not detailed that in her mind; somehow she had seen him as a professional, a man who understood these things and would know what to do. 'I really don't know,' she said.

'I see.' He suddenly sat forward in his chair, becoming very businesslike after the placid, relaxed way in which he had listened to her story. 'Tell me, are you staying in the city?'

'Yes. I took a room at the Sherry. It's where my father used to stay.' She added shyly, 'I'm not very much used to travel.' She did not say it, but her tone implied that only stark necessity could have driven her to make such a trip on her own.

He got up then and came around the desk, giving her a hand to help her from the chair. 'Good. I want you to go back to your room at the Sherry. I want you to have a relaxed evening, a light supper in your room, and early to bed. I'm going to give you something to take that will help you to sleep soundly. Tomorrow morning, say at nine o'clock, I want you to take a taxi to this address; the doorman at the hotel will get the taxi for you.'

He had taken a card from a silver box on his desk, and handed it to her. 'It's a private clinic,' he said.

He saw her eyes widen slightly, and he quickly went on, 'Oh, no, not like the one you were in before, I assure you. This is a medical clinic, quite a pleasant little one. I want to have a few tests performed on you, if you don't object.'

She felt disappointed and put off. She had not come to him for medical advice, despite the fact that he was an M.D. 'I hope you don't think this is all some sort of delusion,' she said. 'There really is something there in the house. I thought you would be able to help me, at least to identify it.'

He smiled, a very reassuring smile, and patted her shoulder. 'We have to start somewhere with every problem,' he said, 'and my form is to start by learning the individual's physical condition. Perhaps it sounds silly to you, but there are various physical conditions that can cause people to, umm, to hallucinate perhaps, to hear things, or see things, even to smell strange odors.'

'But if someone else heard them, too, and saw them . . .'

He was firm, though, in guiding her along the corridor to the little reception room. 'In any case, according to what you've told me, there is nothing to fear until another month has gone by, isn't that correct?'

She nodded; he smiled, and went to a little cabinet. When he came back, he gave her an envelope of capsules. 'This will help you sleep, but only one a night, please. I'm going to set up an appointment for you tomorrow morning at nine. My nurse will call you to remind you, if you like.'

'No, I always waken early.' She let him steer her toward the door, but there she hesitated. 'Doctor,' she said.

He tut-tutted her with his finger. 'Miss Wren,' he said, 'there is nothing for you to worry about. You did the right thing in coming to me.'

'Do you think everything is going to be all right?' she asked timidly.

'Yes,' he said, and ushered her out.

Any annoyance that she might have felt in being so firmly dismissed was offset by the sense of relief that she felt from his assurance. He had sounded so sure, so very certain, that as she left the building she felt as if a great burden she had brought into it with her had been left behind in the doctor's office.

Her relief bordered upon elation. When she came into the lobby of the Sherry and the elevator man greeted her by name, she actually smiled back at him, and said, 'Good evening.' Nor did she eat in her room, as the doctor had advised. She went instead to the little restaurant off the lobby, and with the friendly assistance of a waiter, ordered a very hearty dinner for herself. After all, she had been through physical examinations before. No doubt she would be starved for the next day or so, and like the condemned prisoner, she was entitled to eat a good meal.

She laughed a little to herself, which made a couple at the next booth turn to look oddly at her. Not a condemned prisoner, she corrected her thought; a reprieved prisoner.

She really did feel that way. Someone was interested, someone was going to help her. He had told her she had done the right thing in coming to him, and he had not thought she was crazy.

Wouldn't it be funny, she thought, if everything, all of that horror, had been nothing more than a bad liver? She started to giggle again, and had to put a hand over her mouth to keep from attracting the attention of the couple in the booth. At the waiter's suggestion, she had had a cocktail, something called a bacardi. It was delicious and exotic-tasting, and she felt a little giddy, although whether from the cocktail or her feeling of relief, she could not really say.

Someone was going to help. And he was a medical man, a doctor, not some crackpot.

And he had believed her.

* * *

Alone, in the office she had left, Doctor Buckley was reading over the brief notes he had made. Miss Wren had certainly been extraordinary. It had been a long time since he had personally become involved in the research of a psychic phenomenon; but he did mean to investigate this one himself. At the very least, it would make an interesting story to tell the other members of the society.

He asked his nurse to see if she could reach a Doctor Ida, at the Villa de Valle.

CHAPTER NINETEEN

Helen woke from a deep sleep feeling astonishingly well rested. For an entire evening and night she had been freed from the weight that had been upon her; the pressure that had mounted with each month of her dreadful experiences; the grief, and even guilt, at Robie's death, still not satisfactorily explained. She had actually forgotten these things through part of the evening, and for the first time in weeks her sleep had been undisturbed by nightmares, and those agonizing long periods of wakefulness that had come upon her in the wee small hours when, exhausted, she had nevertheless pursued sleep in vain for hours.

By eight she was dressed and ready, and well before nine she had arrived by taxi at the little building with the address the doctor had given her. It did not look like a clinic at all; it was a little house in the village, narrow and tall, and giving an impression that it leaned out over the sidewalk in a mother-hen gesture that she found somehow welcoming.

The doctor was not there when she arrived, but she was clearly expected. She gave her name to the matronly woman behind the reception counter, and was at once escorted by a starched-uniform nurse to a pleasant, bright room on the second floor, facing the rear, where she could see a tiny garden enclosed by brick walls.

'This will be your room,' the nurse said, as if welcoming her to a new boarding school. 'Please make yourself comfortable, the doctor will be with you in a few minutes.'

It was not Doctor Buckley who came to see her in a few minutes, but another man, who asked her some questions and made some notes on a medical chart.

After that, she was examined. For three days she was poked and prodded, pinched and drained, turned upside down and inside out.

She did not mind, though, because at least she felt that something was being done, however futile it might be. Someone was interested. Doctor Buckley came each day to see her.

Nor was he merely being polite. Helen Wren had fascinated him, and he watched the results of her tests with interest. He did not really think they would find a physical cause for her problems, but it was a possibility that had to be investigated. There were many physical conditions that could produce forms of hallucination, and he had frequently lectured that these probably accounted for many famous 'ghost' legends. Any condition that affected the brain and the sensory perceptions could theoretically produce hallucinatory experiences.

He knew that Doctor Ida at the Villa de Valle had performed a cursory examination of his patient and found nothing significant, but Doctor Buckley was suspicious of any but the most fastidious examination.

'The girl's a little unbalanced,' had been Doctor Ida's advice. 'I wouldn't say she's crazy, but I wouldn't exactly say she was all right, if you know what I mean,' he had said over the telephone.

'I don't think I do,' Doctor Buckley had replied. But he had been unable to solicit any more helpful information from Doctor Ida.

Helen's examination, however, provided him with no physical explanation for the difficulties she had experienced.

'It isn't my liver?' she said with a grin the day he came to discuss the results of her examination.

He smiled in response. In the time since she had first come into his office, Helen had relaxed a great deal. He had been surprised to discover how much prettier she was than he had first realized, and how charming. Freed to some extent from fear and the strain she had been undergoing, she could smile easily now, and talk quite pleasantly.

'Basically you're in good health,' he said, his eyes scanning the reports, although he had already gone over them in detail. 'Your blood pressure is a bit high, but that's to be expected with all this excitement. You're a little anemic, a bit debilitated, of course. But nothing major.'

She made no comment, but waited in silence for him to continue.

He paused and then looked directly at her. 'I'd like you to get some rest. If possible, I would like to keep you here for a few weeks, where you could be given a great deal of attention. I must in all fairness point out, however, that this is not the most inexpensive hotel in the world, if that is important.'

'I can afford it,' she said. 'It will be nice to be pampered for a while. But what are you going to do when—when it's time again?'

'With your permission, I plan to go visit this house of yours. I'd like to spend the night, and see what I can see.'

'You have my permission, of course. You won't want me to go with you?' She looked a little unhappy at that prospect.

He gave his head a firm shake. 'Absolutely not. I want you to stay right here, where you can be watched. Oh, and I will need a letter to your housekeeper, explaining that I will be staying overnight. I won't need her assistance, though.'

'You'd never get it,' she said. 'She refuses to stay in the house at night. Sometimes I wonder if she didn't hear a few things herself.'

'It is possible,' he said. 'In any event, I'm quite used to roughing it.'

He had started from the room when she said, 'Doctor?'

He hesitated and looked back.

'Do you believe there was something there?' she asked. 'Or do you think I imagined it all?'

'I believe there was something there,' he said. 'Exactly what I won't know until I have investigated it further.'

He went out, leaving her to lean back against her pillow and wonder what his investigations would uncover.

* * *

It was not an unpleasant period of time for her; if she could not be said to be ecstatically happy, at least she was free of a large part of her anxiety. For the moment at least it was out of her hands and in Doctor Buckley's, and as far as she was able to do so, she followed his advice not to worry.

She was not confined to her room at the clinic, but could move about freely. She made a habit of visiting other patients in their rooms, and made friends with several of them, much as strangers on a ship will. She knew that she would not see them again after they left this place, but for the present it was nice to be accepted for herself. Here she was not crazy Helen; here no one seemed to know that she was different.

She spent some time in the little garden, despite the cold weather, and she was allowed to have her meals in the dining room in the basement if she chose. It was a bright, cheerful little room, and she was happy to eat there.

All in all, she did not mind being where she was. She was more comfortable than she had been in a long time.

She was there nearly three weeks before the next full moon. There were no calendars in her room, and the one in the lobby downstairs did not show the phases of the moon, but she seemed to know by instinct when the day arrived. As before, a feeling of gloom came over her. Myriad questions haunted her: What if the doctor decided she was a fraud, or crazy? What if something happened to him, as it had happened to Robie? It would be her fault, wouldn't it?

She voiced these fears to him when he came to see her that afternoon, but he only smiled at them.

'I'm capable of taking care of myself,' he assured her. 'This isn't the first such experience I have investigated.'

'When will you go down to the house?' she asked.

'Shortly. I've arranged for you to have an early dinner and a sedative right after.'

'Is that necessary?'

'Very. Sometimes an individual creates an emotional atmosphere in a place. I don't want to take any chance of your thoughts influencing me, even at a distance.'

'You will come to see me first thing

tomorrow?' she asked anxiously.

'I will be here first thing, probably soon after you awaken,' he assured her.

When he was gone, she thought how confident he was, and how much confidence he gave her. She wondered how she had ever thought him pallid or weak-seeming. She saw now that he was very strong; it was a relief to lean upon him for a while.

Not too long after he had gone, her dinner was brought in to her. It was very good, as all the food here had been.

'At these rates,' Doctor Buckley had said when she had commented on this before, 'they can afford to hire an excellent chef, wouldn't you say?'

When she had eaten, a nurse brought a syringe and gave her the sedative the doctor had promised her. She drifted off into a pleasant sleep, completely free from care.

* * *

When he left her, Doctor Buckley went straight to his apartment and prepared for the drive. He wanted to be there well before evening; there was equipment that he would want to set up special photographic equipment to photograph any spirits, or physical intruders, who might appear, and perhaps even some that did not appear. There were photographs purported to be of ghosts that the photographers themselves claimed not to see.

In addition to photographic equipment, there would be recording equipment at several locations to capture any sounds. Miss Wren's story had been of an aural haunting rather than a visual one.

Other instruments would record any changes in temperature, to record, or deny, the chilling cold she had reported. There were less sophisticated devices to reveal any trickery that might occur.

Simply as a matter of routine, Doctor Buckley went armed with Mace. In more than one instance he had investigated hauntings that proved to have been arranged by very human people for motives of their own, perhaps to frighten someone, or for profit, or merely as a lark.

He did not think that was the case this time, but it could not be overlooked as a possibility. Miss Wren was an extremely wealthy woman, he had verified that fact himself discreetly; there were relatives who apparently resented her wealth, there usually were. It was within the range of possibility that one of them might try to frighten her out of her wits, or even want to do her bodily harm.

While he made allowances for every possibility, he had no preconceived notions as to what exactly he would find. He had been through this often before, and in all but a few rare instances he had found nothing.

Sometimes he attributed this to an overworked imagination on the part of those who had claimed to see things before; other times he was willing to admit that perhaps the fault was in him, or even in coincidence. It was possible that a haunting occurred in a house, but not at the time he was there; he would deny no possibility.

He did not believe that Helen Wren herself was engaged in any sort of trickery. That she may have imagined her 'ghosts' was possible, but he did not consider it very likely. He had his own theories as to what had happened, but for the present he did not dwell upon them. Just now he was a scientist making an investigation; it was true that the field he worked in was less well formulated than others, but it was a science nonetheless.

He thought of Helen, asleep by this time, heavily sedated so that not even in dreams could her imagination conjure up a ghost for him. That this sometimes happened he had no doubt. A person with a vivid imagination and also with the ability to communicate telepathically could certainly cause someone else to see a ghost as well. He had no way of proving this idea, but he was convinced of it regardless.

She was a pathetic creature, this Helen Wren. She at once inspired the protective instinct, perhaps because she was so vulnerable, and perhaps because she herself was so indoctrinated into the role of being protected that she fell automatically into that stance.

It was a pleasant drive, once he was out of the city. Her directions had been very explicit, and he found the house without the slightest difficulty. Somehow, stopping briefly as he came up the drive, he had the feeling he had been here before, that he already knew this house. It seemed as if it were waiting for him.

His own imagination working overtime, he wondered? Miss Wren's vivid descriptions? Or was it some sort of telepathic communication?

The housekeeper was expecting him. Again he had a sense of familiarity, as if he already knew her. He thought of the imitation Helen had done of her dour disposition, and barely repressed a smile. She was a grim creature who made no pretense of making him welcome.

'So you're here,' she said. 'Miss Helen wrote to say you would be coming. I for one can't think why you would want to.'

He ignored that pointed invitation to explain his presence. 'I hope I won't be too great an inconvenience for you,' he said.

She led him to the guest bedroom that had been made ready for him. 'I can't stay overnight,' she said emphatically. 'You're going to be on your own till morning.'

'Surely you don't think I need be afraid,' he said.

She gave him a suspicious glance, and said,

'There's been bad things happen here. I guess you must know about them.'

'That was well over a year ago,' he said.

Her only answer to that was a grunt. She had not been informed of the real reason for his visit, which annoyed her, and he did not seem to want to reveal it now, despite the curiosity with which she looked at him from time to time. She showed him where the bathroom was, and how to find his way down to the kitchen.

'That will be fine,' he said, thanking her.

'I won't see you again until morning, then,' she said.

When she had gone, he went to his car and began to bring in his equipment. There was quite a bit to do, but he did it with the quick efficiency of much practice. Evening was upon him, night would soon fall; when it did, he wanted to be ready for anything that fell with it.

First, he made a quick inspection of the house. He snapped photos of the bedrooms that had been Helen's father's and her mother's. If there were any changes in these rooms by morning, the film would reveal them. Just now he saw nothing out of the ordinary in either room. They were two pleasant, rather pompously furnished bedrooms.

The search of the rest of the house was rather cursory. He doubted that anyone was hiding here, although that had been known to happen.

As he went from room to room, he sealed each window and each door to the outside with thread, so that there would be evidence if anyone came in during the night, however stealthily.

He set up photographic equipment and sound equipment in the foyer downstairs; the rest of that would be installed upstairs, however, where the activities had seemed to occur. Cameras and tape recorders were placed in Helen's bedroom and her parents' bedrooms. Nothing could occur audibly or visually without leaving some trace.

Other equipment was set up to record on a continuous graph the temperature in Helen's bedroom, and outside the door to her mother's room.

Finally he went along the halls, both downstairs and upstairs, walking backward and scattering a heavy layer of talcum powder on the floors after himself. No one could walk this way without leaving footprints.

At last, his preparations complete, he retired with a book to Helen's bedroom. He made himself comfortable in the little upholstered chair. He had brought a thermos of hot coffee; he would not sleep the entire night. He did not want to be confused between dreams and waking, as sometimes happened.

Having thus made himself ready, he did what he always did in these situations, which was melodramatic, but nonetheless seemed to prepare him mentally for what lay ahead.

'Let the haunting begin,' he said aloud, in a booming voice.

CHAPTER TWENTY

It was an eerie feeling to wake without having been aware of falling or being asleep. It seemed to Helen that she had only blinked her eyes after dinner, and it was morning, and the sunlight was pouring through the window, spilling gaily over her bed.

It was the first time since she had returned home from the Villa de Valle that she had slept through a night of a full moon without feeling any terror or anxiety.

With that thought, however, some anxiety returned. She wondered what Doctor Buckley had experienced. He had told her he would be here first thing in the morning; what if he didn't come? What if something had happened to him? She would have that on her conscience, too.

She had hardly finished breakfast before he was there, tapping lightly at the door before letting himself into the room. He looked, was her first thought, a little haggard; the truth was, he had stayed up the entire night. He always did that, to avoid any possibility of confusing dreams with reality.

'You slept all right?' he asked her.

'Like a log. I can tell you didn't, though.'

He smiled and said, 'I stayed up the entire night. I'll be going home when I leave here, to catch up on some sleep. I knew you would be worried, though, so I came here first.'

When he stopped, she said, 'Oh, please, don't keep me in suspense. Tell me what happened. Was it like I described it?'

'Some of it was as you described—the house, the rooms, your housekeeper.'

She said, impatiently, 'But what happened?'

'Nothing,' he said. He paused, and then went on. 'Nothing at all happened.'

* * *

He came back late in the afternoon to see her again. He looked more rested this time, although the dark shadows still remained under his eyes. He was nearly fifty; the effects of staying up all night were not so easily erased now as they had been a few years earlier.

Helen was dressed, and she had already informed the girl at the desk downstairs that she would be leaving the following day, and would like her bill made ready.

She had been despondent since Doctor Buckley had spoken that terse word this morning: nothing. Nothing had happened in that house, during the night of the full moon.

She had been made to look a fool, a liar perhaps, or even crazy. She felt cheated and helpless.

'I understand you're planning to leave,' he said when he came in that afternoon.

'I might as well, don't you think?' she said angrily. Her anger was general, but she directed it at him because he was there. 'There's no reason for me to be in a hospital, unless it's a mental hospital. Do you think that's what I need?'

'No,' he said simply.

She had been emptying a desk drawer of the personal effects she had collected in the nearly a month she had been there; she turned to him and said, 'Why not? I must be crazy, don't you agree? I didn't simply imagine those things, they were there. And if you didn't hear them, too, then I must be crazy.'

'I don't agree. I think for your own sake you should find time in the near future to see a friend of mine, a psychiatrist. I think he could help you resolve some personal conflicts in your mind. But before that I think frankly a vacation would do you good. I mean, really getting away from here, away from the area, away from winter. Go to Miami. All that bright sunshine and those loud sport shirts will do you good.'

He spoke with such gentle earnestness that some of her anger was diminished, and she was ashamed to have spoken so sharply to him.

'And what about . . . what about the things that happened to me there? They will happen again when I return—I know they will.'

He pulled out a chair for her. 'Sit down, please,' he said. When she was seated, and he had taken the other chair facing her, he said, 'I don't think you should return there. I think you're right; those things might happen again to you. I think you should sell that house, or give it to some other member of the family. That might resolve some of the family jealousy you've mentioned to me.'

'Then you think—you think there was something there?' she asked. Her voice, and the look on her face, made a plea of it. She wanted to know that he believed that; needed to know it.

'Yes, I think there was something while you were there. The fact that nothing happened while I was there and you were not, does not alter what happened before. Let us say, for instance—this is only an illustration, I am not suggesting this as the explanation—let us say some physical person for some reason was haunting your house, perhaps to frighten you. You were away this month, and they knew this. And probably they knew, too, that I was there. They might not choose to risk haunting the house with a scientific observer on hand.

'I can tell you this, no person came into that house last night. Every door and every window was sealed with thread, easily broken by anyone wanting to come in; but the breakage would have revealed that they had been there. All of the threads were still intact.'

Helen, who had not even considered this possibility, found her despondency vanishing as her interest rose. He had not disbelieved her after all; it was only a question of the right explanation.

'But if someone were already in the house,' she said.

'No. I also put powder around, so that anyone moving through the house would leave footprints. You'd be surprised how many fraudulent hauntings have been uncovered with such simple tricks. But in this case, nothing.'

She looked discouraged, and he said, 'That only proves that no one was there, no physical person. Frankly, I didn't expect that. For one thing, there was the question of what frightened your sister. From what you've told me, she was not the type to be easily frightened. In your case, we must admit that a certain emotional state might have left you more susceptible, but that wasn't true with her.'

'Then you think there were really ghosts?'

'Ghosts is a term not often used by parapsychologists; apparitions is preferable, although I confess the distinction is subtle. But at any rate, yes, I think there was something of that sort, but I doubt that we would be able to establish that as fact without lengthy investigations, and I'm not sure that I recommend that course of action. For one thing it would require your being there, being exposed repeatedly to the same frightening experiences that you have experienced before, perhaps to even worse. I don't think that would be wise. And without that, we can't establish the facts. Where the paranormal is concerned, skepticism flourishes. Anyone who claims to see a ghost is automatically regarded by many people as either deluded, dreaming, drunk, or deranged.'

'I don't care about proving anything to anyone else,' she said, standing again and walking to the window. 'Only to myself. Haven't you any explanation for what happened?'

'Perhaps. It's only theory, of course. No one has yet fully explained apparitions. Two British writers, Payne and Bendit, suggested the psychon, a particle of the mind shed in a house, perhaps at the time of death, that retains enough potential energy to generate a memory picture of the event. Others suggest that every physical thing, be it human or a chair, has a nonphysical counterpart, an etheric object. These etheric objects exist in psychic space, and this sometimes intersects physical space. Can you follow this?'

'I think so. Two worlds, the real world and the looking glass world.'

'Umm, something like that, but without the mirror image effect, the reversing of everything. Anyway, a man's consciousness, his awareness and action, functions either within his physical body, which is the normal situation, or within his etheric counterpart, and a man's etheric counterpart can be projected by a sort of ESP, carrying with it full consciousness.'

Helen gave her head a shake. 'I'm afraid that's too complicated for me. Can you make it simpler?'

'My own idea is simpler, actually, if a little difficult to put into terms. I think that certain events, emotionally powerful events, leave their mark on the psychic atmosphere that exists around us at all times—leaving a psychic stain, as it were.'

'But how would that explain that only I could see or hear these things?'

He reached into his pocket and brought out a billfold, extracting a credit card from it. 'On the back of this card there is printing that is invisible to your naked eye. But if you shone a so-called black light upon it, you would read the letters A-M-E-X. They have been there all the while, but only that light makes them visible.'

He returned the card and the billfold to his pocket, and went on: 'I believe that these stains exist, but they are invisible to most of us, most of the time. But sometimes a person happens along who, for some reason I can't explain, acts as a catalyst, as the black light that makes them visible or, in your case, audible. Perhaps it is because you are on the same emotional wave length, share common vibrations, with whatever happened. You were there that night. Your memory of it must be psychically very similar to what lingers in the atmosphere there. Or perhaps the stain exists about you, in the psychic atmosphere about you, and not in the house. I don't know. But I do think that while I was there last night, the same things were in the atmosphere and were happening as have happened while you were there. Only without your presence, they remained imperceptible to me.'

Helen was thoughtful for a moment. 'Then in one sense,' she said, meeting his eyes, 'I am both the haunter and the haunted.'

'Only in a sense; but yes, I see your point.'

'Then all I have to do is to sell the house; no, your suggestion is better. If I tried to sell it, my aunt might wonder why and make an issue of it. But if I gave it to her, it would appease her.'

'What I think you should do right now is what I suggested earlier—take a nice vacation,' he said. She started to offer an objection, but he put up his hand to still it.

'I know,' he said, 'I know you're frightened of travel, but this is as good a time as any to work on that. I have a friend who runs a travel agency, who could take care of absolutely everything for you. He will see that some-one meets your plane and escorts you directly to your hotel, and takes you anywhere you want to go. I think it would be very good medicine for you. Later, when you've come back, then I think a psychiatrist might be a good idea, just to help with some of the related problems. I recommend Doctor Robert Wallace highly; he's just down the street from me here. But remember that going to a psychiatrist does not prove that you're insane. It may prove just the opposite, in fact.'

After a moment of deliberation, she said firmly, 'All right, I will follow your advice. And I am very grateful for all you've done.'

He went toward the door. 'It was very interesting,' he said.

The truth was, he was disappointed that this situation could not be investigated to a more satisfactory conclusion, but he was equally convinced that to do so would be to expose her to strains that he did not think she could endure in her present state of mind. Perhaps later, when she was better . . . It was as intriguing a haunting as he had run across in a long time.

'Doctor,' she said as he was going out, 'I just thought of something. If I was responsible for making things . . . happen, or at least to be heard to happen, if I am the haunter and the haunted, why, then I must be responsible for

Robie's death.'

Her statement startled him, because it was one he had not anticipated.

'I don't see that at all,' he said a bit sharply, and went out; but he knew that he had not sounded altogether convincing.

* * *

She lingered in the clinic at Doctor Buckley's suggestion until the travel agency had made all of the preparations for her forthcoming trip. Everything was made as painless as possible for her. A man from the agency, as soft-talking as the doctors at the clinic, came to her room and discussed plans with her. They agreed that Florida was nice this time of year, and far enough away to make a good trip without going to too distant a place. When she informed the man that he need not worry about the expenses, he was even more courteous and helpful than before.

A week later she flew to Miami. She had never been there before, and she found it enchanting after the winter gloom of the past few months in New York.

Even travel was not so terrifying as it had been for her. Doctor Buckley's friend took very good care of her. Whenever she wanted to go sightseeing, there was a car and driver waiting at her beck and call. For the rest, she stayed near the hotel and ate her meals there.

By the time she had been there a week she found herself getting around quite nicely without the need of the car and driver, and with no more assistance than some directions or some friendly advice from someone in the hotel. It was a new feeling of freedom that she had never experienced before.

She even began to think of doing some more travel. There were countless places that she had dreamed of visiting in the past, without being able to do so. Now she could see them all if she wished. She could spend the rest of her life traveling if she chose to do so, and she need never face returning to that house. Let it rot, for all she cared.

She wrote to her Aunt Willa to tell her that she had decided the house should have gone to her, and that she planned to take the necessary legal steps when she returned to New York. That, she knew, would still any doubts Aunt Willa had about her.

It was not until the moon began to wax that her nervousness began to return. She knew that she had nothing to fear this time, that for once the full moon would shine upon her without bringing that terror.

Even so, she was tense and out of sorts as it approached, and she knew that she would be grateful when it had come and gone.

It was pointless to plan anything for that night; she knew she would be able to think of nothing else. She stayed in the hotel and had an early dinner in the dining room. The waiter—Joseph was his name—had waited on her since her arrival, and because she looked so lonely, he had taken a friendly interest in her.

'You weren't hungry tonight?' he said, removing the plate with her almost untouched dinner.

'I'm a little tired,' she said, giving him a smile just faintly edged with worry. 'I think I'll make an early night of it.'

'Full moon tonight,' he said, pouring her coffee. 'Very romantic. Good-looking young girl like you ought to be out dancing, or strolling on the beach with a beau.'

She shivered at the reminder of what night it was, and said, 'Maybe next month.'

'That's what you need,' he said. 'A nice beau.'

It was not much after eight o'clock when she went up to her room, but she had a headache, and she really did not feel well.

'It's the worrying,' she said to herself, and she took a sleeping pill and went directly to bed.

She did not know just how long she slept, but it could not have been too long, because when she woke she was still groggy from the sleeping pill.

For a moment she did not know what had awakened her. The room was silent except for some faint noises along the corridor. An elevator opened and closed.

Then it came again, the laughter that had penetrated even her drug-inspired sleep and roused her from its depths; the laughter that had haunted her again and again in the past; the hysterical laughter of her mother's death night.

Her horror was unimaginable. For a moment she sat up in bed, as if frozen in place, and that horrible laugh rose higher and higher, seeming first to come from this direction and then from that.

Hardly knowing what she was doing, she leapt from the bed and half ran, half staggered to the light switch by the door, flooding the room with light.

She had thought perhaps it was a dream, and that with full waking it would fade. But the laugh went on, exactly as she had heard it before, a hysterical wail rising higher in pitch as it gained in volume. Surely, surely, she thought, it must rouse the entire hotel.

She was by the chest of drawers with its gilt-framed mirror, and in the glass she saw her own reflection. She would hardly have recognized herself, she had aged so much. To her own frightened eyes she looked ten, perhaps twenty years older than she was; the illusion was heightened by the disarray of her hair and clothing, and by her wild-eyed look. Even so she would have taken the image for someone else, someone older.

For a moment she stood there, staring at this reflection that was hers and yet not her, an image out of time, and in her ears rang that awful laugh.

It had followed her. She was a thousand miles or more away from that house, and the cursed laugh had followed her.

She did not know just when she became aware that something was moving behind her. She had her back to the bed and she did not recollect any sound in that direction. But instinctively she glanced into the mirror and her eyes were at once fixed by what she saw.

She saw the figure of her father rise up from the bed in which, a moment before, she had been sleeping. He was dressed in shirt and trousers, as he had been the last time she saw him, the night of his death.

He slid over the end of the bed and with two or three swift, silent steps came to stand behind her, with a death-like scowl upon his face. He stood for a moment almost touching her, and in that moment their eyes met in the mirror.

She knew that she was looking into death, into hell.

He lifted a hand around her. He meant to touch her. Whether he did or not she did not know. Heaven mercifully intervened and with a sigh like that of a lover she sank to the floor in a faint.

PART FOUR

DOCTOR WALLACE'S NOTES

CHAPTER TWENTY-ONE

Helen Wren was haunted. That was the point of the whole story.

'Doctor,' she said, before she said anything else, 'I am haunted. By ghosts.'

It was little wonder, too, after what had happened to her.

The truth is, this is not my story to tell. I did not enter into it until it was nearly played out. I met that unfortunate creature only once, and never saw inside that house in which she had experienced such terror and such unhappiness.

True, the role that Fate had assigned me to play was a crucial one, and if I had played it as directed, some tragedy might have been averted.

I say 'might have been'; I believe that I could have cured her of her delusions. Who can say? That is, after all, both the glory and the downfall of man, that he sometimes fails to adhere to the rather simple roles that his creator offers him.

But it is a story that very much wants telling, and who better than I, a professional man, to whom the story, or as much of it as we are ever likely to know, was entrusted, should tell it? I, who can perhaps too late sympathize. How many times, since the afternoon that unhappy woman sat in my office and related her story, have I started from sleep, ears straining for . . . for what? Something unheard, unfelt, and yet perceived, something that chills the marrow of the bones.

How many times, unnerved by a feeling of 'someone there,' have I turned and almost seen something, someone, just beyond the corner of my vision, just—but only just—out of sight? Man may scoff and scorn, but no man lives without some secret dread that may steal upon him in the dark, in the night, in the very form that will most strike horror in his heart.

Helen Wren was haunted by death and by the dead. Every man is haunted, and no ghost is more terrifying than one's own.

* * *

She came to my office on a Tuesday afternoon. It was only by the sheerest chance that she found me there; five minutes more and I would have been gone, would have spent that Tuesday afternoon as I spent every other Tuesday afternoon: hospital rounds, which were brief, because I had few patients in the psychiatric ward at Doctors' Hospital; golf with Milton Taylor; and finally, early cocktails and dinner with my wife on the one evening of the week that we set aside inviolably for one another.

I was already clearing the last of the morning's mail off my desk when Grace came in, closing the door after herself and looking altogether guilty. For the latter she had good reason, which she quickly revealed.

'There's a patient waiting to see you,' she informed me. 'A Helen Wren.'

'I see. And does this Helen Wren have an appointment?' I asked.

It was a rhetorical question. Grace had been receptionist and secretary in my office for almost twenty years, in which time no one had ever had an appointment on Tuesday afternoon; not ever.

I had been in the process of stacking some papers to give Grace before I left. I went on with my sorting. I had already decided—indeed, it was so automatic it could hardly be called a decision—to tell her to tell Miss Wren to return the next day.

Grace, however, did not answer my question directly. She said, 'I think you ought to see this patient. I don't think she would come back to keep an appointment. She seems rather beside herself.'

'About what?' I finished with the papers.

'She says she's haunted.'

I said, 'Haunted? By God. In what way haunted?'

'Haunted. By ghosts. Like the lady of Blackwood Hall,' Grace said. I had stopped fooling with the things on my desk.

Of course she was right. I couldn't pass that one up. I had dealt with hallucinations before, and illusions of various kinds. But I had never actually had to cope with ghosts, despite a fascination with that subject ranging back to my earliest childhood. For some strange reason, that is not a problem people bring to a psychiatrist. I had never even thought of treating anyone for ghosts, but the thought no sooner entered my mind than I was intrigued by it.

'Call the hospital,' I said, refusing to acknowledge Grace's triumph of judgment by looking directly at her, 'and ask them to have someone make my rounds for me. And show this Miss . . . uh, what's her name . . . ?'

Grace was nothing if not tactless. 'I've already called the hospital,' she said, going out. 'Her name is Wren.'

She was back in a moment, ushering in the visitor, and ushering herself quickly out again before I could say what I was thinking.

'This is Miss Wren,' she said, and was gone.

I acknowledged the 'introduction,' adding, since Grace had not thought this important enough to explain, 'I'm Doctor Wallace.'

I suggested that Miss Wren have a seat in the chair facing my desk. Most patients make some remark about the lack of a couch in my office, in place of which I have a large reclining chair. The reason for the lack of a couch is to be found in the very fact that most patients ask about it. The psychiatrist's couch has been an object of so much speculation, humorous and otherwise, that its use is likely to be more of a hindrance than a help. I have my stock answers ready, therefore, when a new patient comes into the office.

Miss Wren did not ask the questions, however. She took the chair I had indicated, hurrying to it as if to a sanctuary, and sliding down into it in such a manner that the back and the arms practically hid her from any view but mine. And I say 'sliding' deliberately. The woman seemed to lack a certain quality of solidity. I might almost have been willing to believe that *she* was a ghost.

Lest I be accused of hindsight, I have consulted the notes that I made during that initial meeting with Helen Wren. The very first notation that I made on the scratch pad that I keep on the desk before me was the word *furtive*, and after that, *haunted*; I had underlined the latter.

Laying aside any consideration of ghosts and visits from beyond the grave, which I prefer to do, Helen Wren's description of herself still seemed remarkably apt. She did indeed seem haunted. No one could look at her and not remark at once the strain that she was under, nor fail to see in her eyes the flickering gleam of fear. I should have said that she was a woman living on the brink of terror.

A comparison came into my mind at once. After the war, as a young army doctor, I had occasion to interview certain Jewish persons who had been persecuted by the Nazis. Although by the time I saw these individuals they had already been released from captivity and presumably from their persecution, they one and all still had about them that look of anxiety, of awful expectancy. They were waiting for something dreadful to occur, something from which, despite all assurances, they were certain there would be no escape. Perhaps nothing done by the Germans against the Jews was more terrible than this, the striking of horror so deep in the heart that it must forever leave a scar, forever haunt the victim.

The woman who had seated herself across the desk from me had very nearly this same look of horror about her, horror beyond hope.

I had made also a note of her name, and added a question mark because it seemed to me that it sounded vaguely familiar. Later, when she had talked, I recollected some of the story concerning the death of her parents; it had made rather splashy headlines for a time.

All of these observations had been made in the course of the few seconds that it took Miss Wren to come across the office and seat herself.

When we were facing one another across the desk, and I had made the notes that I have remarked upon, I spoke to her.

'Now then, Miss Wren—it is Miss, is it, and not Mrs. or Ms.?' She smiled, not a very cheerful smile, and nodded. 'What seems to be the problem?'

'Doctor, I am haunted. By ghosts.'

She had sat with her hands clasped in her lap so tightly that I could see the knuckles were turned white; her eyes lowered.

'I want to be committed,' she said.

'You mean, I suppose, to a mental institution?'

Again she nodded.

'I see. Perhaps it will help if you tell me about this—this haunting. Let me just get some information down here. Will it embarrass you to tell me your age?'

'I'm twenty-seven years old,' she said, and without pause she added, 'I'm a virgin.'

I tried not to show my surprise at her age. I would have guessed it at nearly twice that figure. Now, at a second glance, I could see that what I had at first taken to be signs of her age were only further evidence of the strain under which she had apparently been living.

As to the other remark, I was at once curious as to why she had considered that information germane. I have long held the opinion that there is no such thing as an irrelevant remark. Every remark is relevant to what is going on inside the mind of the speaker and is thus a clue to his thought processes. If the doctor is very fortunate, and is able to accumulate enough such clues that patterns begin to take shape, he is able, in effect, to 'read the mind' of his patient. This, when all is said and done, is what psychiatry is about, Freud and his early toilet training notwithstanding.

In the brief pause that followed, I got the impression (I may have been mistaken) that she expected me to question her further along those lines, but for the moment I had other ideas.

'Perhaps if you told me about this . . . haunting . . .' I said, letting my voice trail off expectantly.

For a moment she said nothing. Finally she said, 'Doctor, if I tell you, you will decide that I'm crazy. It would save time if you simply had me committed now and were done with it.'

'That may be so,' I said, 'but that way you would deprive me of material I need for the book I am going to write when I retire.'

I was a little disappointed that she did not take this as a joke, but seemed to be giving it serious consideration. Be that as it may, she did decide to tell me her story.

I have tried herein to reconstruct that story, more or less as it took shape for me while she talked. I did not take copious notes, trusting to my memory, but I think her story made so vivid an impression that I am not likely to have forgotten much of it. I have a tape recorder in my office on a table behind where Miss Wren was sitting, but when she began so abruptly to talk, I feared that it might distract her if I were to get up to get the recorder, bring it to the desk, and hook it up; and I thus chose not to use it.

But I think I have gotten the story right. She did not tell me her tale in exact chronological order, and there were some points on which she remained vague, so that the reader may see for himself the questions that I had to ponder upon as the story unfolded; perhaps the reader's conclusions will be different from mine (as were those of Doctor Buckley, whom I subsequently contacted).

CHAPTER TWENTY-TWO

Not only did I not make my rounds at the hospital that afternoon, but I did not have my golf game, and I was late arriving home.

Helen Wren's story was fascinating. It was hardly necessary to prompt her, and in fact I spoke almost not at all. Once she paused and asked if she might have a glass of water, and I asked Grace to bring her one. I must give Grace credit, that she had stayed as well, sacrificing what should have been her own afternoon off. She had only a husband to go home to, however, and not a golf game.

'If you are tired,' I said to Miss Wren while we waited, 'please tell me so, and we will continue this another time.'

She gave her head a shake. 'I am tired,' she said frankly. 'But waiting until another time will not help that. No, I would rather go on.'

She seemed to remember herself suddenly, and turning about in the chair she said, 'Oh, perhaps you have other patients?'

'Tuesday is my free afternoon,' I told her. Grace brought the water in a paper cup and I took it from her and brought it to Miss Wren, seating myself once again behind the desk.

Miss Wren was silent for a moment; then she said, 'I have money, you know. I can pay for your time.'

'We won't worry about that just now,' I said.

She smiled—I fancy with a bit less tension than before. I think I had put her somewhat at ease. After another pause, she continued her story. In the telling, I think she was able to relieve herself of some measure of the awful anxiety she carried about with her. She looked more at ease as the time went along.

When she spoke of the incident in the hotel in Miami, however, she grew visibly agitated. She sat forward in her chair and at one point reached out to clasp the edge of my desk, as if afraid of falling. Her eyes grew so wild looking, her whole demeanor so frantic, that I actually felt alarmed and considered interrupting her.

This mood of agitation reached a sort of climax, as it were, when she talked of the vision seen in the mirror.

'I fainted,' she said, and with that, her

shoulders slumped and she leaned back once again in her chair, almost as if she were imitating the faint for me. I thought that the crisis was past, although of course she remained tense and distraught.

She was silent for so long that I thought our interview had probably come to an end. Nonetheless I prompted her by saying, 'And when you regained consciousness, there was nothing in the room with you?'

She fixed her eyes on me again. There was something harsh in the look she gave me; I think she half feared that I was ridiculing her. But my face, apparently, was bland enough.

'Nothing,' she said, dropping her eyes.

'This was last winter,' I said.

'Yes,' she said. 'I haven't been back to New York until now. After that happened, I traveled. I traveled extensively. I couldn't bear to stay in that hotel, and I left the next morning. I could hardly stand to stay in any one place more than a day or two. I began to receive curious letters and telegrams from my relatives, from my aunt, especially. They must have really begun to wonder about my travels. I moved around so much and so fast that some of the letters were weeks late in reaching me.

'I went to New Orleans and Houston and Phoenix, Arizona. To Los Angeles and San Francisco and Denver and Chicago. And finally I went abroad. I went to London and Copenhagen, and to Athens.'

Again she paused for a long time, so that I said, anticipating what she was going to tell me, 'And did these experiences follow you?'

She sighed and it was as if all hope of peace was passing from her through her lips.

'A month after that incident in Miami—on the night of the next full moon—I was in Phoenix. It was quite a distance from home, further than I had ever traveled before, and I ought to have felt safe there. But as the time drew near, I began to feel really scared. I told myself not to be a damned fool, but I couldn't help myself. I was afraid those things had followed me, and I knew if I heard those screams in Phoenix, I would go on hearing them all my life. I don't think I'm completely without courage, Doctor. But there are limits to what flesh and blood can endure. I thought I would go stark raving mad if I heard those cries again. As the time came closer, I found myself counting the days. I could hardly sleep, I had no appetite. I sat in my room, day after day, counting the days. The suspense was awful.

'And one night, about two or three nights before it was due, I was awake, just staring at the ceiling of my hotel room. And I knew, suddenly, that it would come. I was certain of it.

'And it did come. I was more than two thousand miles from that house, and I heard my mother's screams as she was murdered.

'I heard them again in Chicago, and in Athens. And if you can't help me, I am going to hear them as long as I live.'

She stopped. Her long narrative was obviously finished this time. Moreover, with its completion she looked suddenly exhausted, even drained. I found myself wondering how long it had been since she had had something as simple-sounding as a good night's sleep. My immediate impression was that if she could just be reassured sufficiently to allow her a day or two of rest, we would be well on our way to solving her problems.

Afterward I was to berate myself bitterly for taking so simplistic a view. I can defend my actions to myself only by recalling again that there was nothing about Helen Wren to indicate any physical danger. She had seen things and heard things. But nothing physical had happened. Even with that climactic vision of her father, she had fainted before the instant in which he would actually have touched her. And as for that hand which had supposedly shaken her awake at night, she had been asleep. That might have been the effect of a dream, as she herself half suspected.

Moreover, for all her fear and anxiety and strain, Miss Wren did not give the impression of being out of control, or even approaching that state. Considering all that she had been through, I thought her remarkably well-restrained. I think that I myself in her shoes would have been a blubbering idiot by this time.

I did not, therefore, believe in the necessity of actually having Miss Wren committed to a mental hospital. I did feel that she badly needed rest, and of course I planned extensive interviews. But I thought she could get the needed rest in a hospital, in clinical surroundings. She had been confined before, in that first clinic, and then by her Doctor Buckley, and both times had found herself largely free from anxiety or from strange happenings. This often happens; for some persons, who are insecure or beset by anxiety, a clinical atmosphere alone works as a tonic, giving them a sense of reassurance.

It was already late in the day. Whatever arrangements were to be made had to be made at once. It would have been cruel to ask Miss Wren to come back another day when she so desperately sought relief now, and I felt confident that I could give it.

I asked Grace, who still lingered in the outer office, to phone the hospital and arrange a check-in for Miss Wren, and a room in the psychiatric wing.

'I am going to take you to a hospital,' I told Miss Wren when I came back into my office. In answer to the question in her eyes, I added, 'You will be in the psychiatric ward. It is very much the same as being in a mental hospital, except that it is a bit less confining.'

She offered no objections to my arrangements. In fact, when I was ready to leave and she rose to join me, she confirmed my earlier opinion of her physical condition; she looked utterly exhausted.

'How long has it been since you've really slept?' I asked and then, thinking that might be a dangerous subject to pursue at the moment, I said, 'Never mind. They'll take good care of you where you're going, have no fear of that. And the food is good, all those jokes to the contrary. You'll be very comfortable.'

I had no reservations about arranging for her the most deluxe accommodations the hospital could offer. She was, after all, a woman of considerable wealth, and in any event I thought the hapless creature was entitled to some comfort at this stage of things.

In the entire time from the completion of her story until I left her at the hospital, Miss Wren spoke very little; no more, in fact, than was necessary. There was a lifeless quality about her which I attributed to extreme fatigue. I had an idea she had summoned up nearly the last of her resources to bring herself to me and tell her story, and that momentarily at least she was completely exhausted.

The administrator of the hospital is an old friend of mine; for this reason I was able to make short work of having my patient installed in a private room. My questions earlier in my office had elicited the information that her luggage was in a room in a certain hotel, and I had directed Grace to go there, settle up the hotel bill, and to bring Miss Wren's belongings to her.

So when at last I started for home, I thought that everything had been taken care of. If I felt any uneasiness, it was because of that last question Miss Wren had asked me.

'Can't you stay here?' she asked when I was preparing to leave her. 'Just for this one night?'

I smiled reassuringly and patted her hand and promised her that I would see her the very next day. I fully intended to do so. She was, to say the least, a fascinating patient. I was already savoring how I would confound my colleagues with this one.

As I was leaving, the head nurse accosted me to ask if there were any special instructions regarding the patient. I prescribed a mild dose of Nembutal, although frankly I thought that in her state of exhaustion, surrounded by the tranquility of the clinic, she would probably sleep soundly without any help.

'All she needs in the way of medical attention,' I said, 'is rest. Try to see that she is not disturbed.'

This was a psychiatric ward, of course, where some patients tended to be violent, so it was necessary for the nurse to ask if any restriction was called for.

'No restrictions,' I assured her. 'This patient is not violent. Just see that she gets rest.'

I went home.

CHAPTER TWENTY-THREE

All of these activities had carried me through the afternoon and well into the evening. It was later than usual when I finally arrived home. Eleanor, my wife, had been crocheting. She got up from the sofa as I came in, looking a little anxious.

'I thought maybe something had happened to you,' she said, returning my kiss.

'Something did. A most interesting patient,' I said. 'Is there time for a cocktail before dinner?'

'Of course. I have them ready,' she said. She went to the bar and proceeded to pour martinis.

While she was pouring, and I was removing my tie preparatory to settling into my favorite chair, she said, 'I had a strange day myself.'

'Nothing too unpleasant, I hope.'

'Just a lot of little things. Saks delivered the wrong coat—can you imagine that? And I've lost my address book. How on earth can you lose an address book, especially one that big? And Marge Fisher was here all afternoon.'

'That in itself would unnerve me,' I said,

sitting down in my favorite old chair. She brought the glasses across the room, handing me one. I tasted. It was her usual perfect martini.

'Umm, delicious,' I said.

'Thank you. Marge would say it's the full moon. About everything going wrong, I mean.'

She took her own chair and picked up the crocheting she had laid aside when I came in.

I felt an eerie tingling at the back of my neck. I had often heard of that sensation, but I had never experienced it before. I suppose that all men, however highly educated, retain some superstitious inklings.

I looked at her across our living room, and said, 'But it isn't the full moon, is it?'

'Why of course it is.'

'I looked at my calendar when I was leaving the office. I thought it was a whole week off.'

'That calendar on the wall just inside the door? I'll bet you haven't turned a leaf on that calendar in five months. Of course it's the full moon. It's up by now, go see for yourself.'

I did just that. I went to the doors that opened onto the tiny balcony of our apartment, and stepped outside.

Eleanor was quite right. The moon was a round silver disk. It was a trick of the imagination, of course, but I could almost fancy as I looked up at it that those features of its surfaces that appear to give it a face were arranged in an ironic smile.

'Robert? What is it?' Eleanor had followed me across the room, although there was hardly room for both of us on the tiny balcony. 'Is something wrong?'

'I'm afraid so,' I said. I put my martini down on the nearest table and went directly to the phone. It seemed to take forever for my call to get through to the floor nurse in the psychiatric ward. She was a new girl, new to me, at least, and it took a few seconds more to establish my identity.

'I've brought a patient in this evening,' I told her. 'A Miss Helen Wren. I'm afraid Miss Wren is going to require more attendance than I thought. I want her heavily sedated, to begin with.'

'I checked Miss Wren's room quite some time ago,' the voice on the phone informed me, 'and she was already deeply asleep. She seemed to be suffering from exhaustion.'

'I don't care if she is asleep. Wake her. Give her triple the dose of Nembutal. And I want someone with her at all times for the remainder of the night. Is that clear? She is not to be left alone for a moment.'

I could tell from the tone in which the woman agreed that she thought probably it was I who was a bit mad, but I hardly cared what she thought.

I hung up the phone; Eleanor brought me my martini again, and I took a healthy drink from it.

'Robert?' she said.

'Umm, yes.' I was lost for a moment in my own thoughts. I could not escape the feeling that things had gone wrong, past my power to correct them.

I was not surprised then when the phone rang a minute or two later. I think I remained by the phone precisely because I had been expecting that return call.

It was the floor nurse from the hospital. She was calling to tell me that Miss Wren was gone.

'I've no idea where she went,' the woman said. Her voice (probably because she was frightened) had a whining quality that made me wince. 'We're checking the floor now, but it looks as if she's left the hospital.'

'I shouldn't be surprised,' I said. I was mentally cursing myself for every kind of fool.

The nurse waited for some further instructions from me. When it became apparent that they were not forthcoming, she asked, 'Doctor, should I call the police?'

'What? What's that? The police?' The suggestion brought me from the stunned state in which I had been. Call the police? I asked myself silently. And tell them what? That a girl had gotten loose in the city, a girl who was haunted?

'No, don't call the police,' I said. I gave her instructions to report back to me if there was any further news, although I was certain there would not be from that quarter.

'She's gone,' I said aloud when I had hung up the phone.

'Who?' Eleanor asked.

I thought for a moment. Suddenly I snapped my fingers and said, 'I think I know where.'

'Robert, I really don't . . .'

I finished my martini in a gulp and started toward the door. I paused to look back. Eleanor was staring after me, completely bewildered.

'Come on,' I said, getting our coats from the closet. 'I'll explain everything while we drive.'

'Do you think I should come?' she said, already crossing the room.

'We've always spent Tuesday evening together,' I said, and gave her her coat.

It is foolish to hold oneself completely responsible for things that happen to go wrong. Needless guilt is responsible for more of the mental ills that befall individuals than any other problem.

Still, I could not help berating myself as we went. If only I had had a bit of foresight, I would not have left Miss Wren under such casual care.

Fortunately, in the course of our interview I had questioned her about the location of her family home, the house in which these events had taken place. I had not only the address of the house, but a fair idea of its location. It would take at least an hour, perhaps closer to two, to reach it. I was only guessing that this was where she had headed. What we might find when we got there I could not even venture to guess.

As I drove, creeping through the city's traffic as fast as we were able, I told Eleanor the story that I had heard that afternoon for the first time. I had to abbreviate it, and there were certain details that I thought it discreet to omit. But even without these it made an odd tale to tell, racing through the night in Manhattan's raucous traffic, and on the expressway. Above, watching our journey with that mocking smile, was the moon. Again and again I found myself glancing upward through the windshield at that silver countenance. Casta Diva!

'That poor child,' Eleanor said when I had finished my narrative.

'Yes, yes, it's a dreadful story,' I replied. I was looking for street signs. We were nearly there by this time. It had taken most of two hours.

'Robert, tell me something. Do you believe . . .' Eleanor paused. She sounded embarrassed by her question. 'Do you think the ghosts were real?'

'Real?' I found my street and turned down it. 'What is more real than fear, than thought, pray tell me? What in the flesh could be more terrifying than the fears of the mind? She was really terrified, I can tell you that. Blast it.

Where is that street?'

We had come to an intersection. It should have been the one I was looking for, with the street leading up to Helen Wren's house. But according to the street signs, it was not. I stopped at the corner in an agony of indecision. We were close, I knew that. And always haunting me was the fear that I had made a mistake, that she wouldn't be there. It was only a hunch that had brought me to the house in which she had suffered so.

'Robert, look.' Eleanor spoke very softly, which with her always means she is alarmed, and she put a hand on my arm.

I followed her glance. At first I saw nothing. I am used to New York at night, where the sky is ever lighted by an eerie glow, not from the fires of hell, as one might suppose, but from the lamps and beacons of a restless city.

So at first I saw no significance in the glow illuminating the sky in the direction in which Eleanor was pointing. But within moments I came to realize that it was not the steady glow of lighted skyscrapers and movie marquees and electric street lights, but a flickering, sometimes red, sometimes yellow glow.

Just how I knew it was the house that was burning, I cannot say. Perhaps it was intuitive; or perhaps while I drove through the night I had been expecting just such a conclusion as this.

I only know that I did not hesitate, but

turned up the street in the direction of the glow. Following it, I came soon to the walls and the gate that she had described for me. The gates were closed. When I got out to open them, I heard in the distance the keen wail of sirens; someone had already called the fire department.

But they would be too late. I could see that as we drove up the drive to the house and got out of the car. Already the heat was intense, as the fumes leaped skyward from the gabled roof.

I ran to the big front door, braving the heat, only to find the door locked, as I should have known it would be had I stopped to think. I rang the bell, which was scorching hot to the touch, and pounded upon the door shouting Helen's name, all in vain.

Finally, in desperation, I ran around the house to the side. Eleanor tried to run along with me, but she was having a difficult time of it with her heels in the thick grass.

Throughout the scene there was an eerie feeling of *déjà vu*, much as Buckley described to me. I had none of that sense of trying to find my way around a strange property. Rather, it was as if I knew exactly where I was going.

I found the stack of firewood, just where I knew from her description that it would be, and with a piece of wood I broke out the panes of glass in the French doors leading into the den.

But as the glass went, perhaps giving more air to the fire within, a wall of flame rose up before me, blocking any possible entry to the house by that route. I could feel, and smell, the hair burning on my arms as I put them up for protection. The roar of the fire was deafening.

'Robert, for God's sake, come away,' Eleanor screamed, tugging at my arm. 'It's too late.'

She was right, although my mind had stubbornly resisted this truth. I let myself be led back from the house, until we were some distance away on the lawn. I took off my coat, which had been scorched, and wiped the sweat from my face with it.

I started to say something, but Eleanor suddenly cocked her head and said, 'Listen.'

I tried to listen, but at that moment the fire trucks came up the drive, and their sirens drowned out anything else.

'What was it?' I asked.

She gave me a peculiar look. 'I thought I heard someone laughing,' she said.

'For God's sake, where?'

She glanced toward the burning house. 'In there,' she said.

For a moment a cold chill went up and down my spine, despite the heat from the holocaust.

But almost at once my better judgment came to my rescue, and I dismissed the suggestion as impossible.

'You must have imagined it,' I said. The house was by this time an inferno in which no living creature could possibly still survive.

No living creature.

EPILOGUE

Was Helen Wren dead? I do not know. Nobody was found in the ashes of the house, but that destruction was so complete that I do not know if I can cite that as evidence.

So far as I can say, no one has ever heard from her since. I contacted Doctor Buckley, who had not seen or heard from her since he sent her off with his advice to travel.

I discreetly contacted her relatives also, but with no success.

I also contacted the police, but since I felt obligated to respect her privacy and not to tell them the nature of her problem, they did not take my inquiries very seriously. In any event, they had nothing to tell me.

Assuming that she was in the house when it burned, I still could not say what the outcome of that was for her. Whether she ceased to live, or had begun to live with that event, or whether she was still haunted or not, I could not even hope to ever know for sure.

In any event, there is no real evidence she was in the house when it burned. For all I know, she may be living now in some sleepy Mexican village, the true expatriate in sandals and faded bluejeans. Perhaps she has bleached her hair and changed her wardrobe, and with the confidence acquired from liquor or drugs, now mingles in some glittering beach city with the beautiful people. Perhaps they wonder, 'Who is this mysterious heiress in our midst?' Perhaps they call her eccentric. But they neither mind too much, or question too loudly, because she is generous with her food and her liquor and her company, for she is rarely alone.

Only, once a month, she will withdraw. When the moon grows fat and rich in the sky, they will not see her in their lavish haunts. She will be alone then, in the soul's black night, suffering a pain that no amount of drug or liquor can mitigate.

Perhaps—but these are only fantasies that I spin, maybe to ease my own sense of guilt.

There was nothing more that I could do when my investigations, such as they were, found no trace of her. In one sense or another, she was gone. The house was gone. Nothing remained but the ghosts.

And they do remain. Man is born afraid, and dies afraid. So long as man lives, his ghosts will haunt him.

They are himself.